THE LAST DAYS OF

GOOD PEOPLE

PRAISE FOR THE *LAST DAYS OF GOOD PEOPLE*

"With intricate worldbuilding and an exciting, engrossing storyline, A.T. Sayre knocked this one out of the park." —Jonathan Brazee, author of the Sentenced to War and Federation Marines series

"Conservationism in the era of intergalactic travel isn't easy. Sayre imagines rebellion against convention to serve overlooked and vulnerable life, no matter what it costs." —John Wiswell, author of *Someone You Can Build a Nest In*

"An excellent example of 'just when you think things can't get worse.' I had to pause several times as the consequences grew, but found the payoff worth the delay." —Gordon Linzner, founder of *Space and Time Magazine*

"An engaging tale that harkens back to a classic style of space travel science fiction—a wondrous other world, alien contact, real science, multifaceted characters, and a moral dilemma that hits home for today's reader. The writing is smooth and renders the unfamiliar with great imagination and clarity." —Jeffrey Ford, author of *Ahab's Return* and *A Natural History of Hell*

"Sad, bittersweet tale with interesting characters ... This was an excellent story and will be on my [Hugos] shortlist." —*SF Revu*

"A haunting tale." —*Tangent Online*

THE LAST DAYS OF GOOD PEOPLE

A.T. SAYRE

Published by JABberwocky Literary Agency, Inc.

One

EVERYONE WAS PRESENT on the operations deck while Gare was on her conference call with the Ministry back home. Retii Major had just set below the mountain range opposite, but half of Retii Minor was still above the peaks in the slowly reddening sky. It cast long shafts of light deep into the darkened room through the windows facing down into the valley. The shadows against the back wall shimmered and waved like water in the interference from the camouflage barrier covering the windows, masking their presence under the illusion of an unbroken rock face. A line of shadow cut across Gare's closed office door diagonally. Its flutter made Warin think of a pennant.

Warin sat at his workstation, as he normally did, his work pad resting on the desk in front of him. He looked around at the others. Lil, the station engineer, sat at her station across the room, intensely ignoring everyone as she typed furiously onto her pad. Rek had taken the only other chair in the room, lounging at a free station against the back wall, where he sat staring at his own feet. That left Bela and Dav standing, Bela leaning against the wall by the elevator, and Dav by the windows staring out at the alien world, sipping quietly on something hot. Nobody said a word or acknowledged anyone else's presence as the minutes and seconds dragged.

None of them really had much reason to be on the operations

deck, at least not all at once like this. Warin actually couldn't even remember the last time he had seen the base's entire staff together at the same time. Usually it was just the support staff, Lil and him at their stations, and Gare, the commander, in her office. The base scientists, Rek, Dav, and Bela, would make appearances on the operations deck every once in a while: to meet with Gare, to make a maintenance request to Lil or an archival request to him, but other than that, they mostly worked in the field. Even when they were in the base their workstations were downstairs in the lab. But they were all up here now, waiting in tense silence for Gare's call to end. To see what the Ministry's decision would be.

Warin looked down at the two-dimensional map of the planet floating above his holopad. Retii 4. The map showed three continents, officially labeled LM-A, LM-B, and LM-C— which everyone called Llama, Lamb, and Lorca. They were more long than thin, and boomerang-shaped, with each curving inward toward the other two, making a near ring around a massive inner ocean. The gaps between the points of each landmass were not as close as they looked on this map, nor were the coasts so smooth. And there were a scattering of small, mostly uninhabited islands as well that didn't show. But the map was thematic, not topographical. The areas shaded red showed how far among the native population the Bug had spread. It was most of the map. The little continent they were on at the bottom of the world, Lorca, was all that was left that was clear. Or at least, only two-thirds of it was red.

Warin waved through the hologram to close the map. For a moment, he couldn't remember why he had had it up in the first place. Then he remembered that he had been using it to check something in Bela's last report. The numbers had been off on some minor point, at least he thought they might have been—but of course they weren't. He had misremembered. As he should have known. Bela never made mistakes like that. Her grammar could be atrocious at times, but the reports were always very exact. Precise.

He looked over at her leaning against the wall. She stared absently across the room, her arms crossed against her chest. Her face looked calm, distant, as if the moment they were all sharing was boring her. Even as her fingers tapped out some frantic rhythm on her elbows. She must have felt his eyes on her because she turned to look at him. But before he could wave, nod, or even just smile at her, she scowled at him and turned away again.

Warin spun his chair away from her, facing out toward the windows. He was still intensely aware of her presence behind him like heat on his back. He tried to ignore it, staring at the peaks out the window, all but dark silhouettes with the blinding sky of the sunset behind them. But he couldn't focus on them. Or on anything, really. His mind jumped around randomly from one inconsequential thought to another, to avoid thinking about Gare's closed office door and the weighty conversation going on the other side of it. He noticed his right foot tapping on the ground at a frantic pace and pressed his hand on his knee to stop it. Warin sighed. He hoped Gare's call would be finished soon. The mood in the room was starting to get to him.

He got up from his desk and walked over to Dav. The old man had a magnifying panel open on the smart-glass window. He glanced at Warin as he approached, and with a finger he slid the panel between the two of them, gesturing at it.

The panel was set to 30x magnification, focused on the native village in the valley below. Three hundred or so dome-like structures—some small, others quite large, but all single-story. At the top of each dome was a circular hole, some of which he could see wisps of smoke drifting out of. They were arranged somewhat haphazardly in rings around a semicircle of flat common area at the village center, where even at this magnification the natives were little more than whitish smudges going about their tasks.

Warin knew what the natives looked like. He had seen them in the holovids and images that accompanied the field reports the others gave him to file and organize. Their official designation in the reports was DNS-Retii 4, Dominant Native Species—but everyone just called them rettys. They were large, some reaching nearly four meters in adulthood, with long white hair over most of their bodies. They were tripedal, with two large hooved legs pointing forwards and a smaller, third one facing backward that they used like a tail for balance when stationary. Two long, powerful looking thick arms that ended in three digit hands came out of their torso right at the base of their elongated necks, which ended in an oval-shaped head with a long snout, powerful jaw, small nose slits, and three eyes, one on each side and third centered to cover the gap in vision between the other two. Usually the images showed them in simple tunics with little to no jewelry. What adornment they did partake in seemed to be mostly about intricate braiding of their hair, which they would do from head to toe, and could get incredibly complex, involving labyrinthine twists, dyes, and wooden pins. For all their imposing size and alienness, to Warin the images had always exuded a very calm, almost serene-like presence, their long snouts looking almost like they were in a perpetual state of breaking into a smile.

Dav slid the panel down slightly to focus on the fields below the village. "They're just about done for the day," he said to Warin. He increased the magnification. "See them preparing the ground for planting?"

Warin could just make out tiny figures in the fields, swinging some kind of thick staff hard into the ground, dragging it in the dirt for a meter or so, before raising it again to repeat the motion rhythmically. "They're turning the soil like that?"

Dav smiled. "They haven't quite developed the plow yet. As strong as they are, it hasn't been as necessary. Especially around here where the earth is soft. Those staffs have curved blades on the end, kind of like a scythe but angled out to one side. It gets the job done. They'll get that field turned before sundown, and then the one next to it tomorrow while the young start planting in the first. The children will catch up to the adults by the end of tomorrow, and both fields will be planted. Then they take a day, rest, and then move on to plant the next two."

"How many fields do they have?"

"Twenty-four. Though only two-thirds is planted in a given season and the other third left fallow on a rotating basis."

"Wouldn't it be better to keep going, get it all done as soon as possible? Why do they take the day off in between?"

"To let the earth recover before asking more of it."

"What?"

"It's kind of a ritual act," Dav said. "Probably ages ago their ancestors over-farmed their fields and ruined the soil. And the warning passed down to be more careful with how they farm evolved over the ages into the practice."

"That makes sense for the field rotation, but not the stuttered planting schedule," Warin said.

Dav shrugged. "It's what they do."

"And when they're all planted, that's when they have a festival, right?"

Dav glanced at Warin sideways. "So you do pay attention to the reports."

"I read them a little," Warin replied with a smirk. "It'd be impossible not to. Just that if I sat and studied every bit of what you all bring in, I'd never get them filed into the database."

Dav nodded and sipped his drink, staring thoughtfully down at the village for a moment. He continued. "The festival is not quite as big an event around here as it is elsewhere."

"It is just a village down there."

Dav shook his head. "Even in the proto-city upriver it's somewhat subdued compared to the other continents. On most of Lamb, the festival was a week-long affair of music and revelry. One great party. Especially in the bigger settlements. At the trading centers too, even though there was no direct agriculture going on at them. On Llama it was shorter, just the one night on most of that continent like here, but much more intense. They adhered to the rituals as the main focus. Sometimes almost exclusively. There was a village in the northern quadrant where the entire night and following day of the festival was spent in silent meditation. The whole village kneeling together in a semi-circle unmoving for an entire solar day."

"That sounds miserable."

"I thought it was fascinating. I wrote a paper all about the various customs of the planting festival across the planet a few years ago. It'd be in the database, if you're interested."

Warin shook his head. "I don't need that much of a distraction."

"Well I guess I won't go ahead with the presentation on the subject I was going to do for everyone after dinner."

Across the room, Rek chuckled. Lil looked up from her pad and glared. "Do you mind?" she snapped at him. Everyone turned to look at the pair of them as Rek put his hands up in mock surrender and turned away from her. Lil buried her head back in her pad, muttering to herself.

Warin turned back to the window. "Maybe you should think about doing it anyway," he said to Dav under his breath.

Dav shook his head with a grimace and went back to staring quietly down at the village. Everyone else remained silent in their own worlds.

Gare's office door opened with a squeal that was exaggerated in the silence, causing everyone to jump as the base commander stepped out onto the deck. She stopped at her doorway when she saw everyone looking at her.

Bela stood up off the wall and turned to face her. "Well?" she asked. "What did they say?"

Gare turned to face Bela. She started to speak but stopped, instead looking downward, frowning. "The request was denied."

Bela nodded and walked away across the room. Rek shrugged. Warin heard Dav, who had turned back around to look out the window, sigh very deeply.

Lil stood up from her seat. "Just like that? No deliberation, no analysis, the Ministry just turned it down flat?"

Gare put up her hands. "We all argued for them pretty vigorously, all the post commanders. Even a minister or two was with us. But it's a pretty open-and-shut case, Lil. The rettys are barely out of the Stone Age. Nowhere close to advanced enough to authorize intervention."

"Are you going to file an appeal?" Dav asked her.

Gare nodded. "A joint appeal from all observation posts. I told them to expect it as we ended the call. Each of you is welcome to add your name too."

Rek folded his arms across his chest. "Is it mandatory?"

Gare rolled her eyes at him. "Nobody is required to be involved in the appeal, Rek. It's your own choice." She looked over at Warin. "I need you to compile the current stats on the rettys, along with a few other things we'll be filing with the appeal. I'll let you know which reports and get you a cover page for it by tomorrow. Letters from the other observation posts should be coming in to include as well."

Warin nodded at Gare. "Of course."

Gare continued. "But I don't want any of you to get your hopes up over this," she said to the entire room. "It's a long shot. At best. I will do what I can. So will all the other post commanders and staff. But you should all learn to accept that the Ministry's decision is not likely to change. The rettys just aren't advanced enough."

Lil snorted. "By whose standards?" she asked.

Rek cleared his throat. "Considering it's us that would be doing to intervening, ours."

"Yours, maybe," she spat back at him. She turned back to Gare. "What about the culture, the spirituality, the intricate customs, the detailed societal organization? None of that matters? Just their tech? Measuring the rettys based on their technology level is unfair. It's biased. Who cares if they didn't domesticate animals? They're herbivores. They didn't because they didn't need to, not because they can't. There's plenty of other factors the council should take into consideration."

"You know that's not how it works. All of that was taken into consideration, not just the tech level. And more." Gare walked over to the main station in the center of the room. "But it's just not enough."

"Those heartless assholes—"

Warin cut her off. "Lil."

"What?" she nearly shouted.

"You're not helping."

"As if any of you are."

"And what exactly would have us do?" Gare asked sternly. "Hmmm? If you have an idea, we're all listening." Lil turned back to her commander but said nothing. Gare took a deep breath and continued in a calmer tone. "Nobody's happy about this. But the Ministry's decision is final. And we are duty-bound to observe it. We all took the same oath. We're scientists, researchers. Not the arbiters of life and death in the universe."

Lil sat back down in her seat heavily, turning to face the wall. "Just another great day in the Federated Ministry of Science."

Gare did not reply and went back to her computer. Rek got up from his chair with a grunt and called the elevator. The doors opened immediately and he left.

Out of the corner of his eye, Warin noticed the light from the windows increase. He turned back around to see what had happened. Retii Minor was all but gone behind the opposite peaks, and proper nighttime was only minutes away. Yet the world outside was brightening as the mild fuzziness of the view of the valley grew sharper. He turned back to Gare. "The window camouflage is going down," he said.

Gare looked up at him with a nod and back down at her computer. "I'm taking the masking systems offline."

"What? Why?"

Gare shrugged. "It's just a drain of energy now."

"But what if the rettys notice us? The base?"

"It doesn't matter," Dav said to him. Warin looked at the old man. Dav glanced up from the village with a sad smile. "There's no need to hide. We can't influence the rettys' development anymore. They're going extinct."

Two

THE BUG ITSELF was nothing new to the planet. And was not actually a bug but a virus, initially carried by a few species of a specific flying parasitic insect. Or at least the equivalent of insects on Retii, which were more arachnid-like. And the Bug thrived in only one region of the planet; the wet, humid jungles on the southern tip of Llama. It was unable to spread beyond that region, though, being blocked by dry plains to the north, mountains to the east, and the ocean to the west and south. Which had been fortunate for the rettys because the Bug had a near-one-hundred-percent fatality rate for them. Because of that, those Llama jungles were the only area of the planet that the rettys had not spread out to. Any native who wandered into that rainforest rarely survived more than a few days. But as long as the rettys stayed clear of the southern jungles in the tiny little patch of land, and the Bug stayed trapped there, the rettys could continue to grow across the rest of the world, safe from the virulent plague.

Then two planetary years earlier, volcanic activity in the mountains of southern Llama increased dramatically. Which caused the ice in the surrounding peaks to melt at higher rates at the end of winter. Which then flooded into the plains below them, creating pockets of swamp and marshland. Which allowed the Bug-laden insects to break free of the rainforest and spread north throughout the long, hot summer. By the time the weather started to cool, several small villages bordering the plains had been completely wiped out.

It could have ended there, or at least soon after. The cold winters in central Llama should have stopped the Bug, killed off its carrying insects, leaving it to recede back into the swamps from whence it came. That's what the scientists tracking the Bug in nearby observatories had expected to happen. Outbreaks had happened before, a handful of times in the nearly thirty-five years since the Ministry had come to study the planet. Each time it came out raging, only to ebb back to the jungles with the turn in the weather. There was no reason not to expect the same outcome this time.

"But the Bug mutated and jumped species," Bela said, rolling over onto her stomach. "Multiple species, actually. Small vermin animals, a couple of the larger vertebrates. Those flying snakes— that's the one that really spread it. They all became carriers. It killed off a few of them too, but not before they could help spread it everywhere. There was no way we could predict that."

Warin stared down at her bare back next to him in the bed. "Shit luck."

Bela glanced up at him, raising an eyebrow. "Isn't it, though?" She turned her head on her folded arms to face away from him.

Warin got out of bed and slipped on his undershorts. He walked over to Bela's small kitchenette and poured a glass of water. He leaned his back against the sink and drank slowly, staring down at her. She was suddenly oblivious to his presence. Her shoulders rose and then sank as she sighed, her head shaking ever so slightly as she did. She was then motionless. Warin might have assumed that she had drifted off, but he could see a sliver of her eye from his vantage, staring at the base of the lamp on the bedside table next to her.

He swallowed the rest of the water, placed his glass in the sink, and came back to the bed. He sat on the edge on her side by her feet, running his fingers gently on her leg. Bela smiled absently.

"Nine, five, and three," she mumbled.

"What's that?" Warin asked.

Bela frowned. "That was the retty population on the three continents before the Bug. Nine million on Llama, five million on Lamb, and three million on Lorca. Now there couldn't be more than a few dozen rettys left on either Llama or Lamb combined. If that. The fraction of a fraction of a percent that are immune. Lorca's down to nearly a third of that number and the Bug just got here." Bela reached out and tapped on the edge of her bedside table with her finger. "It's just so virulent. I've never seen anything like it in nature. Once it broke out, the rettys never stood a chance." She turned to look at Warin. "Do you know how the Bug kills them?"

"It's a respiratory thing. It clogs up their lungs."

Bela shook her head. "That's a simplistic description. And lung, singular. The rettys only have a single organ for gas exchange which you would call a lung."

"All right," he said. "I'm not the scientist here."

Bela smiled. "I know." Warin said nothing and she continued. "The Bug gets into their system through direct contact with a carrier, either an animal or insect. From there it makes its way into the retty's lung and lodges all over their, well, let's just call them alveoli; it's close enough. Though the rettys' version of them pulls in more than just oxygen like ours, they also pull nitrogen and a few other lesser gases from the air for other uses in the body. It's really a far superior respiratory system to ours. But anyway, once the Bug attaches to them, it starts to siphon off the gases meant for the bloodstream, growing and multiplying rapidly, preventing more and more nutrients from entering circulation. The immune system is always too slow to get involved, because the Bug mimics the chemical signature of the capillaries. So, nothing stops it and soon the body is getting nothing. Outwardly, the retty starts to get sluggish and disorientated. Feverish when the immune system finally goes into action—always too late. Brain function starts to stifle. Every system in their bodies starts to collapse. They grow weak, unable to move, probably in total delirium. And shortly after they first show outward signs, a day at most, they die. Essentially of suffocation."

"Sounds horrible."

Bela shrugged. "There are worse ways. It's painful, maybe. But they're so out of it at that point they probably don't feel much."

Warin shook his head. "Let's not talk about this anymore."

"Why not?"

"It's depressing. A whole species getting wiped out. And there's nothing we can do about it."

Bela turned over onto her back and raised up onto her elbows. She gave him a patronizing smile. "There are three things I have in the lab right now that could've stopped the Bug cold. And I can think of a few others I could synthesize in a day or two. Hell, I could have made a vaccine with an aerosol delivery system in a week, put it in a drone, and flown it over all the towns and villages in this region, and the rettys wouldn't have known anything had happened. Except that they all would've stopped dying."

Warin shook his head. "You know we can't do that."

Bela slid across the bed. "Noninterference, I know. We can't interfere in the natural evolution of the planet. We must only observe and study."

"That's the mandate, Bela."

"I know what Ministry policy is, Warin. I'm in the Ministry."

"So am I."

Bela snorted. "I'm a *scientist* in the Ministry, not an administrator." She got out of bed and walked over to her bathroom. "And one thing I can tell you as the scientist here is that sitting on our hands and watching an entire sentient species die off is not the same thing as 'nothing we can do about it.'"

Bela closed the bathroom door behind her, latching it locked. A few moments later, the shower started. Warin shook his head and started to get dressed.

THE LIGHTS IN the corridor were dimmed to simnight level when he stepped out of Bela's room. He hadn't realized it had gotten so late. After just a few meters down the corridor, he felt a yawn wash over his head and shoulders, suddenly feeling tired. He shook his head. Such a Pavlovian response, he thought. It was like putting a cover on a birdcage.

Rek and Lil were sitting in the galley, talking animatedly, as Warin entered. He hugged the wall all the way to the refrigerator as if the meager extra distance would make a difference.

"All anyone is asking you to do is sign the letter," Lil said.

Rek nodded. "Right. Asking. Not ordering. As in it's voluntary. As in I don't have to sign it if I don't want to. Gare said so herself."

"Yeah, but—" Lil stopped, closed her eyes, and took a deep breath. "Everybody else on the planet is signing it. All the other researchers at all the other observation posts. You're the only one who isn't."

"Well if you have everyone else, why do you need me?"

Lil slapped the table. "To show it's unanimous! God, Rek, all anyone is asking of you is a simple signature. An absolute bare minimum of empathy. I don't understand why you are being so stubborn about this."

Rek leaned back in his seat, rubbing his forehead. "Because I'm not interested in wasting my time with empty gestures," he said. "On general principle."

Lil laughed. "On principle?"

Rek crossed his arms. "It's a meaningless statement."

"It's not meaningless."

"Yes. It. Is," Rek said, emphasizing each word. "When has the Ministry ever changed their mind? About anything?" Rek shook his head. "It's not happening, Lil. Not here. But if you all want to file an appeal, that's fine: do what you want. But it won't change the fact that the rettys don't meet the standard for intervention. Not by any interpretation of the guidelines. It's tragic, but it's the truth."

"So why not just add your name if it's so meaningless?" Lil asked. "What difference would it make to you?"

"What difference does it make to you that I won't?"

"Maybe I hope there was a shred of decency in you," Lil said coldly. "That you could show just a tiny bit of compassion for a whole species that's going to get wiped out."

Rek's jaw muscles clenched. "What I do or do not feel about the natives has nothing to do with it."

"I'm sure all the untapped mineral resources underneath the rettys that you've raved about since you got here have nothing to do with it at all. I mean, screw them, right? They're just in the way of a great profit margin. But once they're gone, there's no more civilization to protect. There'd be nothing stopping whatever mining consortium you'll end up working for from staking a claim. So why bother trying to save them?"

Rek glared at Lil stone-faced for a long time. When he got up from the table, he scraped his chair loudly across the floor.

"Take your sanctimony and shove it up your ass, Lil," he said. Rek turned and stormed out of the room.

Lil stared at the doorway after him and then over at Warin, who had his back to her, stirring a bowl of soup intently on the counter. He glanced over his shoulder at her. "So I guess he's still a maybe," he said.

Lil snorted and got up from the table. "More like a lost cause." She walked over to lean against the counter next to him. "There's just no getting through to some people."

Warin took a spoonful of soup and blew on it gently. "I doubt accusing him like that helped."

"So what? You know it's true. He doesn't care. He's probably happy they're dying. I bet he's been sharing his geological data with one of the corporations since he got here and they're just waiting to move in."

Warin shook his head. "The data's not confidential, Lil."

"But it's not available right away, is it? The Ministry needs to send it through a mountain of red tape first. Takes years before anything about this planet is released to the public. I'm sure the head start would be worth it to one of the major consortiums."

"Come on, Lil. Rek is Ministry to his bones. He wouldn't violate policy like that. He's a lifer. He might be a little disinterested in anything without a mineral makeup, but no way is he chasing money."

Lil snorted. "Says you. I'll bet you anything he'll resign and be back on contract with a mining firm within a year of the last native dying off."

Warin said nothing and took a spoonful of soup.

"You saw Gare's letter yet?" Lil asked after a beat. "She sent it out for everyone about an hour ago."

"I haven't," he replied. He turned to Lil quickly. "But I am signing it before you go off on me for being a soul-sucking bureaucrat."

Lil scowled. "I know you're signing it. I never thought you wouldn't. Because unlike him, you care."

Warin nodded. "But you still gotta accept it, Lil," he said, taking another spoonful. "Rek's right. It's not gonna make a difference."

"Maybe not. Maybe they are beyond being shamed. Might need to do something more." Lil ground her jaw in small circles. "Maybe something drastic."

Warin turned to look at Lil, who was staring at a point across the room. "Such as?"

Lil glared back at him, her eyes narrow slits as she tried to read him. After a moment, she shook herself and looked away again. "Nothing," she said dismissively. "Never mind." Lil pushed off from the counter. "I have some maintenance to deal with in the basement." Warin watched her as she quickly hustled out of the room.

Back in his quarters, he sat down at his desk and switched on his pad. It was still remote-connected to his workstation on the observation deck. He had been so surprised when Bela had called him he hadn't even bothered to shut it down. It was a breach in protocol, leaving his station unattended while logged in, though one nobody would likely find out about— or even care that much if they did. Lil did it all the time at her observation deck station and Gare never said anything. She especially wouldn't care now with what was on everyone's mind.

He stared at the screen, shaking his head slightly. Rek's latest report. A geological survey of the inner ocean shelf off of Lorca's northern coast. Warin scrolled through it quickly, reading only a few lines here and there, and as such he barely followed any of it. He shook his head and closed the file. He could finish reviewing it tomorrow. There was no rush.

Warin scratched his scalp. Lil was planning something. He knew it. Maybe she wasn't fully clear of what that was just yet, but he could see it in her eyes back in the galley that she wasn't going to just sit back and do nothing. And she had almost told him, he thought, but she had stopped at the last moment. Which was fine by him. He wanted no part of whatever dumb and pointless gesture she was planning. Whatever it was it wouldn't work, and it wasn't worth getting in trouble over. Leave him out of it.

He closed the connection to his workstation and opened his inbox. There was a long message from his sister. She was still not pregnant, which he knew after the first few lines. Otherwise she would have led off with that news instead of the goings-on at the office job she had that he only vaguely understood the dynamics of. He'd read it again and reply to her tomorrow.

Below that was the internal message from Gare with the cover page for the appeal attached, asking for everyone to read it over carefully and reply to her if they wanted their name included on it when the report was filed. Warin opened the attachment and started to read it, but after just a few paragraphs he closed it again and dropped Gare a quick note agreeing to it. He was sure whatever it said was fine. It still didn't matter.

It was just those two messages, though. Still no response to his transfer request. He shut off his pad and leaned back in his chair. Five galactic years was the standard assignment length for a Ministry bureaucrat, but eighteen months was not unheard-of. It was considered bad form or a possible sign of serious issues to request transfer earlier than that, so he had waited until the very day he had been on planet long enough to put in for his without raising eyebrows. That had been weeks ago and he had heard nothing. It might have been too late by then. What with all that was going on, the Ministry might not want to cycle in new personnel now.

Warin would take anything, though. Another backwater planet. Inventory clerk on a Sol system reclamation barge. Even data processing back at central looked better than here. The mood at the post had been slowly deteriorating for over a year now, growing worse as the fate of the rettys grew more certain each day. And then the final decision from command yesterday—he could already sense how morale had gone right off a cliff.

Why did he have to stick around for it? The others, they were the biologists, the xenologists, the geologists, studying alien planets and the life on them was their calling. They had to be here, it was their job to document the retty's fate. Hell, even Lil was integral in keeping the base running. And Gare was the commander. He was just the data analyst. He had taken the same oath the rest of them had, fine, and he believed in the Ministry's philosophy just as much as the rest of them, but so did plenty of others. Anyone could do his job; it didn't have to be him.

Warin rubbed his face hard. He wanted nothing more than to avoid all of the dread that was coming out of every seam in the place now, to be as far away from here as he could as soon as he could, before death came sweeping down from the hills and into the valley.

Warin got up from the chair and flopped down on his bed without getting undressed, only kicking his shoes off onto the floor absently. He was getting ahead of himself. His transfer hadn't been denied yet. And maybe it wouldn't be. Maybe they would let him go someplace else. Maybe they'd want to get new people in here early to prepare for the shift in focus after the extinction event. It made a certain kind of sense to him that they would. After all, his workload was bound to slow down quite considerably. Most of the research was over now. So it might be the perfect time to let him transfer out.

He was able to calm himself down enough to drift off to sleep with that hope, and starting to vaguely imagine where he would go once he was free of this planet and its doomed natives.

Three

THE AIR TASTED like menthol. Or at least that's what Warin thought as he exited the jeep. He took several deep breaths, walking in a small circle as Dav locked down the vehicle behind him. They had stopped inside in a small clearing in a clump of trees roughly halfway down the mountain, and were surrounded by thick forest on all sides. Sunlight only came through in small patches on the ground, but it was not particularly dark; more comfortably shaded.

The colors would definitely take some getting used to. There was green in the leaves above, and in some of the weed-like plants that grew at the base of the trees, but there was far more blue, white, purple, and yellow in the flora around him. The ground beneath his feet in the small clearing was covered in a flat, porous-looking purplish moss that had a glossy sheen as if it was covered in oil. It felt springy under his feet and bounced back quickly from his weight when he lifted his foot. Nearby there was a long-overturned tree whose surface was covered in bright yellow clover-looking plants. And from the underside of the deadwood shot chalk-colored stems, curving around the shape of the ancient trunk into the air, ending in blue, square-shaped leaves that dripped down under their own weight. Most of the rest of the ground between the large trees was covered with a reddish knee-high or taller brush that stood in patches and walls, looking thorny and impassable.

He didn't see any animal life, at least nothing larger than a handful of insects perched here and there or flying around. The jeep's approach had probably scared off most of it. He could hear them, though, both in distant, echoey cries and chirps barely audible above the hiss of the wind through the leaves, to others that were seemingly closer. The collective sound of it all felt almost overpowering after so long living with nothing other than the hum of the station as a background. Something large cried out, a high-pitched, wheezy sort of sound, clearly far away but still cutting through the air sharply. Warin jumped at it, grasping at the pistol holstered on his hip and looking around furtively. He saw Dav behind him had stopped and turned to glance at him over his shoulder. The xenologist shook his head reassuringly and turned back to the jeep without a word.

Warin relaxed with a sigh and walked up to look at one of the trees more closely. It was large, at least three meters in diameter, with bark that was more red than brown, and thin with a light, almost fur-like covering. His eyes rose slowly up the trunk to the branches that started about six meters above his head. Dark green finger-like leaves in bunches of six or so fluttered as the wind picked up briefly. The branches themselves all bent back from their base as if to wrap around the main body. He saw the same twisting direction of the grooves in the trunk, as if the tree was spinning around like a top.

He reached out to the tree but stopped before his palm touched its surface.

Dav came up to stand next to him. "It's all right," he said. He reached out to the tree and rubbed his hands on the furry trunk brusquely. "It's actually helpful. It's how they spread their seed. Animals brush against the follicles as they pass by, and they either get caught in the air and float away or get carried away on the animal." Dav stepped away from Warin and clapped his hands in front of him, looking away. A cloud of white sparkled in a shaft of sunlight next to him.

"It's pollen?" Warin asked, looking up the trunk of the tree. "For something this size?"

"Not pollen. This is asexual reproduction. Seeds. Very tiny ones." Dav looked around at the forest with a smile. "Each of these massive things was once just a bit in a cloud of dust."

Warin shook his head. "You're kidding me."

"There are trees back on Earth that do the same thing, or similar at least. It's not all pine cones, chestnuts, and acorns. I mean, I don't know of anything off the top of my head that goes from microscopic to the size of a great oak, but still." Dav walked back to the jeep, where he had rested two sets of packs against the back wheel. Each had a solid ceramic case for storage of delicates, with other nylon pouches strapped to the top and bottom. He grabbed one of the sets with a great grunt and slipped it on over his shoulders. He hopped in place to adjust it more comfortably on his shoulders. "Come on, we should get going. We're burning daylight."

After an initial circuitous route around ditches and thick brush, they came upon a vague animal path heading farther down, just wide enough for them to walk single file. Warin was sweating profusely and breathing hard by the time they found it, but kept quiet because he saw no signs of strain in the older man ahead of him. His footfalls started to become unsteady, and he stumbled on a tree root and bumped into Dav.

The older man turned around and grabbed Warin by the shoulders to steady him. "Easy there," he said. "Let's stop here for a moment. Take a break." Dav slid Warin's pack off his shoulders and rested it on the ground between them. He guided Warin to the base of a tree to rest and then kneeled in front of him, carefully examining Warin's face. "Feeling a little light-headed?" he asked.

Warin nodded. "It's nothing."

"It's the air. Take a tablet."

Warin furrowed his brow. "I took one when we left."

"Take another one." Dav reached into a pouch on his belt and held one of the little white oblongs up to Warin's face.

Warin took the tablet in his shaky hand and put it in his mouth. It tingled slightly as it dissolved on his tongue. His mouth filled with an icy-cold liquid, which he kept swallowing until the tablet was completely gone.

"First time out in this atmosphere is always hard," Dav said, removing his own pack and sitting down cross-legged. "Your system has too much difficulty getting oxygen out of the air. It takes a while to fully acclimate. We'll take a quick break here while we wait for the oxygen tablet to get into your bloodstream."

"Is there a reason we didn't drive all the way there?" Warin asked, still panting.

"I didn't want to drop too much on the rettys all at once. We'll be alien enough for them without showing up in a shiny magic cart. Besides, I thought you'd appreciate a walk in the outdoors after being stuck inside the post for so long."

Warin scoffed. "That's very considerate of you."

Dav waved his hand at him. "It's only a couple of kilometers. And it's all downhill. You'll be fine."

Warin rested back on the tree behind him and looked up its trunk. The cover above was thinner here than where they had parked, and he could see more of the sky. Small clouds, thin and with an odd yellowish tint to them, rolled through the greenish-blue sky. Retii Major was not quite directly above; it was more off to his right and very large, easily the size of his fist out at arm's length.

"I need you to accompany Dav tomorrow," Gare had told Warin back in her office.

"Accompany him where?" Warin had asked.

"Down to the village in the valley. With the noninterference protocols lifted, he wants to take the opportunity to study the rettys through direct interaction."

"He's allowed to do that?"

Gare shrugged. "Without the protocols in effect, there's nothing to stop him. They're not a viable species anymore, so there's nothing to preserve."

Warin sat forward in his chair. "So we couldn't interact with the natives at all to avoid contaminating their society and development, but now that they are on the brink of extinction, we can stroll down and say hi?"

"Basically."

"That sounds like a flaw in the guidelines."

"More of a loophole."

"I'm not sure I see the difference," Warin said. "What if the rettys actually wind up surviving the Bug? What then?"

Gare shook her head. "According to the studies done on planet, there's less than one half of one percent chance of that. Analysis back at the Ministry confirmed it. That's a main reason the protocols are not in effect."

"This doesn't sound to me like a very good idea. Why are you letting him do this?"

"His seniority allows him a good amount of latitude on the scope of his research."

"So he pulled rank on you."

"That's not what I said," Gare said, shaking her head a little too much. "Dav has over forty years in the Ministry—fifteen on this planet alone. I expressed my concerns about this expedition to him, officially, but he promised he would be cautious.

And with as much time in the Ministry as he has, and with his stellar record, well, that gets him a lot of trust that he knows what he's doing."

"I don't know. It just feels like there are so many things that could go wrong with this."

Gare waved her hand. "Like what? The fate of the natives is a foregone conclusion. So why not let him meet them before they die off? There's no harm in indulging him. Or at least it's not worth trying to stop him."

Warin let that go. "So why do I have to go with him?"

"Because nobody else is free and I don't want him going to the retty village alone."

"Ah," Warin said, nodding. "You want me down there with him in case one of those things that can't possibly go wrong goes wrong. Is that it?"

"There's no reason to think there's any danger at all, Warin," Gare said with a sigh. "The rettys are fairly passive and they score very low on the xenophobe chart. And Dav is confident he knows enough to make contact."

Warin smirked. "But he doesn't *really know*, does he? He's never been around one of them. Nobody has. It's all theory. I'm not trained for self-defense, Gare. What good will it be for me to be along if they start chucking spears, except to be another target?"

Gare rubbed her eyes. "Look, I know this is not in your job description, so I can't really order you to, but could you just go with him? It'll be perfectly fine. There's no reason for concern about Dav going to the village, but I still don't want him or anyone in the field by themselves. Normally Bela would go with him, but she's apparently working on something she can't take time away from in the lab. Lil and Rek are also busy. Your workload is pretty light right now and not about to pick up any time soon." Gare looked away from him at the pad on her desk. "Besides," she continued almost offhandedly. "It would look good on your record to log some time in the field."

He knew that last comment was because of his transfer request. She had never talked with him about it, but of course she knew—the moment the request had arrived at the Ministry, they would have forwarded it back to her for comment. That was standard procedure. And considering his relatively short time on the planet, what she would have to say could have a lot more weight than normal. She probably couldn't block it out-right; at least, he couldn't see her expending the effort needed to do so. But she could respond to it in such a way as to make it reflect very poorly on him for asking out early.

Warin scratched his ear. He couldn't really see her doing that. Gare was not a malicious person and they had always got-ten along well. She had to understand why he wanted to leave and that it had nothing to do with her or her command. Why would anyone want to stick around for what was about to hap-pen if they didn't have to?

She could just let the transfer get buried in her other work, though, not acknowledge it in any way. That could delay it for a while. She probably had been putting it off, at least a little, not wanting to deal with it with everything else that was going on. Or conversely, she could also move it to the top of the proverbial pile and expedite the process. In return for a favor from him. Like accompanying Dav to the village even though it wasn't in his purview.

Which is why he was here now, gasping alien air and leaning against a furry tree.

Of course, he also could have been reading far too much into that one little comment. Seeing subtext that wasn't there. It was entirely possible. But it wasn't a chance he wanted to take. Anything that he thought could get him off this planet sooner, he would do. Even something as ironic as going deeper into it.

WARIN'S DIZZINESS HAD completely dissipated after a few minutes. He started to sit up against the tree, grabbing the water flask off his belt to take a small drink. Dav noticed and got to his feet. "You feeling better?" he asked Warin.

Warin took a few deep breaths and felt no discomfort. He picked himself off the ground and stood. His legs felt solid underneath him and his head felt clear. He brushed himself off, nodding to Dav.

Dav smiled back. "Okay," he said as he picked up his pack, turning to continue on the trail.

The path led out of the trees down a short, sudden incline and into a field of knee-high, purplish, reed-like vegetation that looked to stretch all the way across the valley of lazy hills to the mountains on the opposite side. There was no sign of the village yet, but if his grasp of the area from watching the valley up at the observation deck was reliable, it should be behind the collection of hills ahead to the west.

Warin tilted his head upward and closed his eyes. He had to admit the warmth of sunlight on his face did feel nice. He had spent the majority of his childhood in space stations following his parents' careers, so being inside the observation post continuously was not a problem for him. But direct, real sunlight was something that hadn't even occurred to him that he had missed. He wasn't even sure when he had last felt something like it. Before the posting on Retii he had been on an orbiting platform above Novum, a toxic and uninhabitable rock mined for osmium. He definitely hadn't visited that planet. Not that the sulphuric atmosphere and crushing pressure would have been pleasant if he had. There was the hiking trip on Reticulae a girlfriend had talked him into, but now that he thought about it, he wasn't sure if that was before Novum or on leave just after he was posted there. It was a long time ago, either way.

And that had been a terraformed planet, full of Earth-based flora and fauna. Little more than a planetwide, carefully crafted and maintained garden. A park. This place was nothing like that. This was his first time in a truly alien biosphere. In real nature. He turned around himself as he followed Dav. It went on in all directions. True wilderness. He hadn't so much as seen an animal beyond someone's pet before without there being a magno barrier between them. But out here, one could come loping up or charging at him at any moment. He smiled. Strangely enough, the thought of it didn't panic him. It invigorated him. It made his senses feel sharp.

Dav turned back to look back at Warin as he continued walking across the field. "So listen, I know I can count on you not to do anything stupid, but when we get to the village, just follow my lead, okay? The rettys are friendly, but still, I want to strike just the right tone. So let me do all the talking."

"I thought they didn't talk," Warin said.

"A figure of speech."

Warin nodded, thinking. "The reports all say the rettys use nonverbal communication. So like, sign language?"

Dav shook his head. "Not so much, no. There is some of that, of course, just like we have, but their language is in the face and eyes—gestures, blinks, tensing and releasing of facial muscles. Microexpressions."

"Are they deaf?"

"Their hearing is fine. At least no worse than yours will get when you're my age."

"All right." Warin adjusted the straps on his pack and stretched out his neck. He continued. "Communicating through expressions like that sounds kind of limiting. At least for a primary form of communication."

Dav chuckled. "Not at the level they use it. Their visual language is just as detailed as any of our own. The intricacy and subtlety of it took years to decipher." Dav paused for a second, glancing off into the distance. "The rettys have amazing vision. Beyond having three eyes, which gives them an almost-three-hundred-degree view, they also have more than twice the number of optic nerves as we do in each eye. And a larger portion of their brain is used for interpreting the stimulus coming from them. The average retty's eyesight is probably better than 30/01 compared to ours. Maybe even more. They can see minute details that our eyes and our brains can't even register. So it only makes sense that they'd develop nonverbal communication as they evolved. They do have a rudimentary verbal language too, for use over distance, or in pitch black, or any time a visual sightline is not clear. Which is how we'll be able to talk to them. But it's not their primary form of communication."

"Okay," Warin said. "So that's what we can use to talk to them, but we're not going to be able to understand everything they say back?"

"I have something for that, don't worry."

"If you say so," Warin said dubiously. "Is there anything else I should know?"

"That depends on what you know now," Dav replied with a shrug.

Warin shook his head. "Well, assume I haven't retained much from your reports on them. Or read back to things filed before I was assigned here."

Dav smiled. "All right. The basics, some of which I suppose you know. They're herbivores, asexual, a mostly agrarian civilization, though with some forays into mining and seafaring—though not around here. They score respectably well on the sapience scale and low on the aggression scale."

"So, friendly farmers."

Dav nodded. "Basically."

"What about written language?"

"There are a few, but it's not widespread. It's mostly for accounting in the larger settlements. Most of their history is handed down orally—or I should say, visually in their case. Probably only a handful of the rettys can read anything at the village below."

"Do they have money?"

Dav shook his head. "Barter. When necessary, which isn't all the time. They're more of a collective society."

"Religion?"

"They don't really have any."

"No religions?"

"No. Or at least not what you would consider a religion. They have a reverence for the land, which makes perfect sense for a farming community, but it doesn't seem to have a mystical component to it as such. It's more utilitarian. They don't personify nature or see omniscient entities in the stars or clouds. Nothing like that. The closest they come to it is in their stories and myths, which have gotten embellished over the generations with some interesting events. But it's never developed further than that."

"So no gods? No afterlife?"

"It doesn't seem so."

"What do they do when someone dies?"

"When a retty dies, they're planted in the farmland. So they can continue to feed their family. And as far as we can tell, that's it."

"They use them as compost?"

"Well fertilizer, but yes. I told you, Warin. They're utilitarian." Dav was quiet for a moment, then continued. "I don't want you to get the wrong idea about them, that they lack imagination, are simple-minded. Because they aren't. They are very creative people. They do a lot with sculpture, weaving, painting, jewelry, and the stories they tell each other, as I mentioned. They have art. They don't have music, strangely enough, but that's probably because they are more visually orientated than even we are. But they do have creative minds. Even the intricate way they braid their fur, and dye it, and bind it with combs, pins, and things like barrettes—it's very expressive. Wait until you see them. It's just for whatever reason, that imagination was never used to try and explain the natural world around them."

"Why do you think that is?"

Dav furrowed his brow. "I have some vague ideas. But it's one of the things I hope to learn more about from direct contact. There's only so much you can learn about a species—"

Dav stopped suddenly, staring to the east. Warin followed his gaze. A dark blotch grew slowly larger in the distance, appearing to be heading toward them.

Warin walked up next to Dav. "What is it?" he asked.

"It's a herd," he said, still watching them.

"A herd of what?"

"A local herbivore. Grazers. I don't remember their classification. I just always think of them collectively." Dav started walking again at a slightly hurried pace, not taking his eyes off of them. "It looks like they're on a run."

Warin followed him. "A run?"

Dav shook his head with a scowl. "They have an oversensitive flight instinct. Gets set off at anything. If one of those things steps in a hole the wrong way and jumps in surprise, it's liable to start a chain reaction through the whole herd. Then the whole mess of them start running."

"So what you mean to say is a stampede."

Dav shrugged. "If you want. I just don't like the connotation of that."

Warin could hear a low rumble coming from the herd, just on the periphery of his hearing but getting louder. "I don't think word choice is the issue here, Dav. They're coming this way."

"I am aware of that," Dav said. He pointed to a set of bumpy hills a couple hundred meters away. "That's why we're heading for there."

The herd kept getting closer as they made their way to the hills. The rumbling sound grew louder, and inside it Warin started to hear sporadic, high-pitched bleats of individual animals. The sound of it made them both hurry their pace. Halfway to the hills, they were close enough for Warin to get a good look at what the animal was; a thick, tubular thing, just a shade darker purple than the grass around them, with a flat horizontal head ending in an oval mouth, just below a triad of eyes that looked wide-eyed and wild, their heads jerking around sharply in all directions as they pushed themselves along on two powerful digitigrade legs. They were top-heavy, so much so that remaining upright was not sustainable on its own, and they would occasionally stumble or start to lean forward as they ran. When they did, another single front leg would reach out from just under their long necks and push their body upright again, then go back to tucked tight against their upper torso as they ran. As best as he could tell from the closing distance, they weren't very large, either, the biggest being only what he would guess was the size of a large dog, though most were half that. But collectively there were hundreds, maybe thousands of them heading their way.

The two men were still a few meters from the hills and running when the first few leaders of the herd started to whiz past. The rumble and cry of the beasts were deafening. Warin had to dodge more than one of them that ran past to avoid colliding with it. He was sucking in air very heavily again, and his limbs were starting to stiffen and grow clumsy under the exertion. He was honestly shocked at how easily the energy had left him, forgetting completely in the moment that he still wasn't acclimatized to the air.

Warin was starting to slow down, the sweat heavy on his brow. He could see Dav ahead, already climbing up the side of the hill. After a few meters safe above the run, Dav stopped and turned around to look back at him. He waved his hands encouragingly, shouting something Warin couldn't hear over the roar of the animals.

The herd grew thick, almost impassable, and Warin found himself unavoidably kicking and getting his legs tangled up in the ones that crossed his path too close, nearly falling down over and over. Soon the animals completely surrounded him, so thick he couldn't see anything below his waist. He tried to use his size advantage over them as much as he could, but the throng of them pushed against him like a strong water current. It got even more difficult the closer to the hill he got, as the herd split around the rise and the mass of animals bottlenecked against the side of it, growing thick in front of him.

An animal slammed hard into his back, pushing him forward onto his hands, and he scrambled back up as quickly as he could. He fell again after a few steps. His calf got stepped on as he tried to get up, sending him back down. Another animal hopped over his head, kicking him in the ear. They all started to run over him. He covered his head with his hands. There was a constant rattling sound of their feet connecting with the hard case on his back, like heavy hail or stones hitting a roof. Most of them were small and did not hurt him as they passed, but an occasional heavier footfall on his legs or arms sent a sting up his spine. A musty panic filled his nose, both theirs and his own. He let out a loud yell and clawed with one hand blindly forward underneath them all as best as he could toward the hill, hoping he hadn't gotten turned around in all of this.

My first wild animals, Warin thought.

He vaguely heard a series of loud pops nearby and smelled something acrid. The footfalls on his body stopped. He opened his eyes again and looked around. The animals over him had inexplicably scattered, cutting a wide circle around his area and pushing themselves behind him deeper into the herd. Some kind of blue smoke hung in the air nearby.

Free of the burden of them on his back, he shakily got back onto his feet and stumbled the remaining distance to the hill, where he climbed up to the waiting Dav on his hands and knees.

Dav took off Warin's pack for him and laid him against the hill. "Are you okay?" he asked.

Warin sat up a little, breathing heavily. "I think so." He stretched out his arms and neck slowly. He saw little scratches all over his body but no real bleeding. His shirt and shorts were covered in dirty marks and stretched and frayed at the edges. "Mostly just sore and out of breath. Nothing broken, I think."

Dav sighed in relief. "That's fortunate. A colleague stationed over on Llama got caught in a herd once. They got three cracked ribs. Those things are small and light, but all together in a herd it can be pretty rough."

Warin nodded. "Yeah. I think I'd say calling it a stampede is accurate."

Dav laughed. "Fair enough." Dav looked back down the hill at the herd still rushing past. "Come on, let's get to the top of the hill."

Warin walked up the steep hill slowly, with Dav supporting

him with an arm under his armpit, carrying Warin's pack on his other elbow. By the time they reached the top, he felt good enough to walk on his own and took his pack back from Dav, carrying it in front of him by the straps. He reached into his pouch on his belt and pulled out a tablet. "By the way," he said, popping it into his mouth. "Where did you get the fireworks?"

Dav turned to look at him. "The what?"

"The fireworks. Whatever it was you threw at the herd back there."

Dav looked at him. "I didn't throw anything at them."

"Well, something made them scatter. I just assumed you threw something at them. Some kind of exploding repellent. You're saying it wasn't you?"

Dav shook his head. "When I saw you go under, I started scrambling back down to try and pull you out. Next thing I know, they dispersed around you. I've no idea what made them do that. I thought it was just the random herd movement."

Warin stopped and turned to face Dav. "I swear I heard a bang, a few of them, and saw a cloud of smoke in front of me."

"Well it wasn't—" Dav stopped suddenly, looking with surprise over Warin's shoulder. He turned to follow where Dav was looking.

The top of the hill was a wide and mostly flat ridge, flat enough for some larger flora to take root. Various almost flower-like plants twisted and weaved into each other before giving way to a small grove of narrow trees that came out of the ground at various awkward angles.

Standing between the flora and the trees less than five meters away was a retty, leaning forward on a staff they held in their hands, staring directly at them.

Four

THE RETTY MADE no move toward them. Their thick hands gripped the staff they leaned on loosely, their digits fidgeting as they appeared to adjust their grip. They turned their head side to side, bringing each of their side eyes to bear down on the two of them in turn.

The native was dressed in a tan sleeveless tunic with a bulky satchel of some sort draped across their body. All much like the garb Warin had seen in the reports. But the retty's things were more ratty and old-looking and had dark stains that had long since faded into the fabric. The retty themself looked to be older. Their fur was thin and spotty, and what there was of it was pulled back into fraying braids that looped down over their limbs almost like sleeves on their arms. The hair on their neck was loose and frizzled behind them with only a few wood-en-looking pins to hold it out of their weather-worn face. Old, definitely. Yet the retty looked in no way infirm. Warin could see the strong muscles of their arms and neck, which twitched ever so slightly when the native moved. But otherwise, the retty looked at ease—relaxed, calm even. Certainly not alarmed in any way. If anything, Warin thought they looked bemused.

Dav grabbed Warin's hand resting on his holster. "Don't," he said flatly.

Warin turned to face the xenologist. Dav looked like he was

resisting the urge to smile. He licked his lips quickly. "Everything is all right," he said to Warin. "No need for the gun. They wouldn't know what it was anyway."

"Dav—"

"I told you. They're not aggressive."

Warin looked at the retty, who still watched them unmoving. "You sure?"

"Absolutely. Just trust me."

Warin let go of his holster and dropped his hand limply to his side.

Dav slowly took his backpack off and laid it on the ground, not looking away from the retty. He fished around inside it for a long moment before he found what he was looking for: a monoaural headset. He glanced down at it as he stood back up, bringing himself to stand shoulder-to-shoulder with Warin.

"What's that?" Warin asked.

"It's a translator," he replied. "The natives are visual, remember? I had to make this thing special for them. It links back to our retty language database up at the station. It should be able to read the retty's face and translate what they say."

"Should?"

"Well it's not like there was a way to field-test it." Dav put the headset on, folding out a microphone and monocle-shaped viewing glass. "I didn't have time to print up more than one of these," he said as he adjusted the glass in front of his right eye. "So you'll just have to follow along for now. Tune your comm to channel four."

Warin tapped the bud in his left ear four times. Dav flipped a tiny switch just above the earpiece, and the viewing-glass screen started to glow blue around the borders. Dav made a few minor adjustments to the glass.

When he was satisfied he was ready, Dav cleared his throat

and put out both his hands in front of him, palms up. He nudged Warin in the elbow and he did the same. "I greet you. I am a friend," Dav said, very slowly and clearly. Warin heard his words on a slight delay in his earpiece. "We come in peace."

A fraction of a second after Dav had finished, a series of odd sounds came out of a tiny speaker on the band of his headset. It was surprisingly loud, having come from something barely the circumference of a fingernail.

The retty blinked hard, all three eyes in unison. They stretched their head down toward the two men as if straining to hear. Dav touched a button on his headset. "Repeat message." He took a few steps closer to the retty. Warin followed behind as the same series of sounds came from the speaker.

The retty raised up to stare down at them, cocking their head to the side. Dav stopped moving forward. Warin took a few steps backward, looking straight up at them. He had not realized how much the retty had been slouching.

"We are friends," Dav said, only the slightest bit of crack in his voice.

The retty slumped back down again, bringing their head level with Dav. From behind Dav's shoulder, Warin saw the retty's face twitch ever so slightly, their mouth open and close, their eyes blink fast, with only an occasional click or chirp.

"What are you, strange creature?" The words came into Warin's earpiece. *"You look nothing like the animals of this land."*

Dav noticeably breathed a sigh of relief. He turned to Warin with a smile, holding the mute button on the headphones. "You heard that?" he asked.

Warin nodded. "Are you sure it's accurate? I barely saw anything for that much speaking."

"You wouldn't. Your eyes aren't good enough." Dav let go of the button and turned back to the retty. "We are travelers.

From far away. We've come to make friends. To learn from you and your people."

The retty cocked their head to the side. Another collection of twitches and blinks. In his earpiece, Warin heard, *"Your face is gibberish. Is that why you shout?"*

"Turn down the volume," Warin said.

Dav muted the headset again. "That's not what the retty means," he said. "Shouting is just anything verbal." Dav unmuted. "We can only shout. We cannot control our faces. They are too... numb."

The retty's head bobbed up and down, almost as if nodding. *"Numb faces,"* they said.

Warin snorted. "Only took a couple of minutes and we got a racial slur." Dav scowled at him.

The retty adjusted their feet. *"What is your family?"*

Dav blinked. "My family?" he mumbled. "You mean— right, my family." He gestured to Warin and himself. "We are human. Human beings. My name is Dav. He is Warin."

The retty looked back and forth between the two of them and walked slowly forward. Warin's put his hand on Dav's shoulder. His other hand went to his holster again.

Dav brushed his hand off. "Everything is fine, Warin. Just relax."

The retty stopped less than half a meter in front of Dav, and held out their staff in front of them horizontally on their upturned hands. *"Well met, Dav human human beings. Well met, Warin human human beings,"* they said. *"I am Tyundelorro, scavenger for Oollaroa. I welcome your friendship."*

Dav smiled wide. "We welcome your friendship." He stepped closer to Tyundelorro and put out his hand. The retty looked down at it. "This is custom of greeting among us," Dav said. "To touch our hands. To show friendship."

Tyundelorro stared at his hand for a long moment, then put out their own next to Dav's, palm facing up. Dav reached out with his other hand and turned the native's sideways and placed it in his own. He shook the retty's hand in both of his.

When Dav released, Tyundelorro held their hand up to their face to look at it. *"Strange custom,"* they said.

Tyundelorro turned to Warin. Warin straightened his posture and stared back with a forced smile. Tyundelorro held out their hand to him. After a moment's pause, Warin trepidatiously reached out his own, and Tyundelorro brought up their other hand to cover his and shook up and down slowly. Their skin was coarse against his own, leathery-feeling. But the native did not squeeze—they barely exerted any force at all. He relaxed and his smile became more sincere. When he looked back up at the retty he could see minor twitches in their face as the native spoke to him. But no translation seemed to be coming from his earbud. *"Insufficient data,"* it finally came out with. Dav's headset couldn't see even a profile view of the native from where he was standing. Warin smiled wider, his jaw muscles tensing.

Tyundelorro let go of Warin's hand and turned back to Dav. *"Is this one dumb?"*

Dav stifled a laugh, badly. "Not dumb. He does not have this." Dav gestured to the headset. "This, uh, headband is a tool. It helps us understand you."

The native poked their hand at Dav's headset. Dav turned his head to give them a better look. Tyundelorro seemed cautious not to touch it, their hand stopping just short of tapping the headphone.

"You have powerful magic," they said, moving back away.

"It is only a tool," Dav corrected. "We have no magic."

"But your tool speaks," Tyundelorro said.

Dav shook his head. "We have no magic. I swear. We are just like you."

"So you say. But I know of no tool that can speak for its master."

Dav started to respond again before Warin interrupted. "I think this is a point we can let go of for now."

Dav muted the headset and turned to Warin. "It's important to make sure they don't see us as gods."

"They don't have gods."

"Well let's not give them any. I want to nip it in the bud right now."

Warin glanced at Tyundelorro, who watched them with that same bemused look on their face. "They just saved me from getting trampled by a herd of three-legged cats. I'm not an expert on alien psychology but I don't think that's going to be a problem."

Dav turned back to Tyundelorro with a shrug and unmuted his headset again. "We are traveling to your village. Is it far?"

The retty pointed over their shoulder. *"Oollaroa is near. Just the other side of these hills there is the road. I should accompany you there. If I am with you, then there will be a proper welcome. But I need to finish my task first, if you will wait."*

"We can help you with your work," Dav said, turning to look at Warin. Warin shrugged, not sure what help they could be to the large creature.

"Your friendship speaks with your offer," Tyundelorro said, holding up their hand. *"Follow me to my cart and we will pull it into the field and load the carcasses."* The retty started off down the side of the hill.

"I'm sorry, did they say carcasses?" Warin asked, as Dav picked up his pack and started after them. "Was that an accurate translation?"

Dav didn't answer and kept going, gesturing over his shoulder for Warin to follow.

Down near the foot of the hill was a wooden cart, which was little more than two solid wheels and a deep basin. It leaned down onto two thick handles in the front that were connected by a pliable-looking strap at each end to make a very basic harness of sorts. Tyundelorro slid their staff into a set of rings along the side of the basin, picked up the cart by the harness, and pulled it behind them around the hill.

Warin caught up with Dav as he turned around the hill toward the field on the other side of the hill. "What exactly is it that we are collecting out here?" he asked the xenologist. "The translator said carcasses."

"It did," Dav said, nodding. He gestured in front of them. Beyond Tyundelorro ahead of them was the field they had crossed to reach the hill. The grass was bent and matted down in a wide swath, torn up and broken in places, though showing signs of rebounding already. In the grass Warin saw little clumps of flesh here and there lying perfectly still.

"The ones trampled in their own stampede," Dav said.

"But the rettys are herbivores. What do they want with the dead animals?"

"For the crops."

"More fertilizer?"

Dav nodded again. "They have a lot of farmland."

"And they use these just like their own dead. I can't tell if this means they think more of these animals or less of their own kind."

Tyundelorro dropped the cart and turned to the two men. *"We can collect enough from here,"* they said, pulling out gloves and a kerchief from their satchel. *"Take only the larger ones and leave the tiny to the vermin."* The native covered their mouth and nose with the kerchief and headed out into the field as they slipped on the gloves.

Warin turned to Dav. "Did you know this was what you volunteered us for?" he asked.

Dav dropped his pack by the side of the cart. "I assumed it was. They called themself a scavenger. And it's a common practice in the villages of this region." Dav rubbed his hands together. "Never thought I'd get a chance to participate, though." He opened his pack, pulled out a pair of gloves, and put them on.

The herd animals were heavier than Warin expected, especially the larger ones, and he wound up dragging them by their legs more than carrying them. To his relief, most of the bodies were not especially bloody; they were warped, broken, and most had a trickle of dried bluish liquid from their mouths and eyes, but only occasionally had the trampling broken their skin and spilled their insides out on the ground. And there were enough of them that he could bypass any that were. There was a smell to the bodies, like a sulphuric musk, and as the afternoon wore on it started to grow more noticeable. He pulled the collar of his shirt up over his nose and mouth to block out as much of it as he could.

Dav didn't act as if he noticed the smell as he worked. In fact, he seemed to almost be enjoying himself. "It's fascinating, you know," he said to Warin, as they carried a larger corpse together to the cart. "The way the rettys use the herds. Watching them, scanning the land to predict the path a stampede would take, and then picking a spot to collect the ones that get killed after they pass by. I bet our friend here actually caused the stampede to begin with, one of those bomb things he used to save you on a timed delay of some sort. It's very clever."

"Yes, very impressive," Warin said.

Dav continued, ignoring Warin's tone. "It's similar to what some of our ancestors would do. Indigenous people in North

America used to chase bison off of cliffs, for example. The bison would break their legs or otherwise be immobilized in the fall, leaving them helpless for other hunters to move in and kill them off. The Europeans called them buffalo jumps."

They swung the heavy corpse back and forth between them in growing arcs, then flipped it over the side and into the cart. It thudded sickly against the other bodies inside.

"I think that's enough helping," Warin said. He took an oxygen tablet as he looked out into the field where Tyundelorro was still collecting. They dragged two larger corpses by their feet in one hand as they made their way towards a third. "With the ones they have right now the cart'll be full."

Dav nodded and took off his gloves, panting hard. He wiped his brow in the crook of his elbow. "Though it's not an exact comparison. Buffalo jumps were traps, either built or an enhanced natural feature, and could take out an entire herd of bison at once. A very bloody scene, I'd imagine. This thing our friend here does is far more passive. And nowhere close to that scale."

Warin stepped downwind and away from the cart. "If they instigate the stampede it's not all that passive," he said.

"True." Dav grabbed a capsule from his pack at his feet and popped it into his mouth. "Still, it doesn't feel like quite the same thing as a hunting tactic, does it? No chase, no direct killing. And they're not run off the land. In fact..." Dav looked around the area. "The herd is pretty much locked into these fields—mountains on two sides, and woods they can't pass the other two. It's almost like this whole area is one large pen they can't get out of. I wonder if the rettys altered the land to keep them in."

"You think that's likely?"

"Over many centuries? It's possible. I don't think anyone has ever looked into it. But if the rettys did, then that would make this a very early form of domestication."

Warin shook his head. "But the rettys never domesticated animals."

"Unless they do and we just never noticed." Dav tapped his fingers on his lips, thinking. "The rettys never had cattle because they're herbivores, so had no need for food from them. And they are physically one of the strongest animals on the planet, so they wouldn't need them for labor. At least, not enough to bother to take generations to tame something wild. They only have this one use for animals, as fertilizer for their crops. Which doesn't take a lot of them, so it's a demand that is easily met with a cartload like this every once in a while. All they need to do is make sure that the source is steady. So the villages and farms around here started trapping them in the fields to provide easy access. And the whole thing didn't get more sophisticated than that because the population is sparse in this region, so it didn't need to. But it's still—" Dav turned to Warin, his eyes wide in excitement. "We're witnessing the very beginning of a major societal development here."

"Dav—"

"Don't you see? Animal domestication. One of the major leaps in civilizational development. We thought they skipped it, or weren't advanced enough for it, but all the fundamentals of it are here in this field. This is incredible, Warin. I know it's small now, but once the practice spreads into the more populated areas of the planet..."

Dav's words trailed off, his eyes locked on the distant mountains over Warin's head. After a long moment, his shoulders slumped, his head bowed, and he let out a deep sigh. "Shit," he said, almost under his breath.

Tyundelorro came in from the field and swung four corpses

into the cart. The native pulled the kerchief from their face and walked over to stand in front of Dav. *"Are you ill?"* they asked him.

Dav looked up at him, plastering a thick smile on his lips. He unmuted the headset. "No, I'm fine," he said. "Just resting. Suddenly felt tired."

"Odd way to rest on your feet. You already have one too few for all your weight." Tyundelorro put their hand on Dav's shoulder. *"I thank you for your help,"* they said. *"You are generous. Now we can head for Oollaroa and I will make you welcome in my home."*

The native walked to the front of the cart and stepped into the harness. The strap fit perfectly onto their upper torso. They turned the cart around to head back toward the road on the other side of the hill.

Warin lifted his pack and put it on his shoulders. Dav turned and watched Tyundelorro as they pulled the cart over the uneven grass, moving slowly, carefully, to prevent it from tipping over.

Warin picked up the xenologist's pack from the ground and held it out to him. "Come on, let's keep up with them."

Dav looked at Warin and nodded quickly. "Yes. Thank you," he said, taking his pack. As he slung his pack over his shoulder, Warin thought he could hear him mumble to himself, "Best-laid plans of mice and men…"

Five

THE ROAD TO the village was elevated from the ground on both sides, made of stones tightly packed with pebbles, all worn smooth from use. Warin guessed it was about six meters wide, or at least large enough for three lanes of carts like Tyundelorro's to travel on unobstructed. It ran in a relatively straight line over gentle inclines of the land to the horizon, only bending to avoid steeper hills or forest. Every so often a path branched off from it, running off to fade in the distance or disappear behind a sharp rise or into a patch of trees, but they were barely more than the trodden grass of common use.

The three of them walked down the center of the road, with Warin and Dav flanking Tyundelorro as the native pulled the cart. Dav had recovered from his moment of melancholy, and he and the native were deep in a conversation of ever-changing content. Each of them took turns asking the other questions, going seemingly from one subject to the next at the whim of whatever came to each of them. Though Warin could sense a certain intent in Dav to maneuver the conversation with Tyundelorro into certain areas very gently, as if he was trying to hide that he was studying the native. Which of course he was. Warin was a bystander to all of it, occasionally looking back and forth between the two of them as they talked, but more out of a sense of politeness than any deep interest. Leaving the conversation by falling a step or two behind them would be too close to the cart that stank in the hot sun.

They did not come across any other rettys in the road at first, but from almost the moment they reached it Warin had seen them—a handful of them in the distance in the fields, or the trees, or up in the hills they passed. Or at least he thought he had. Most of the time it was so far away he wasn't sure. They were barely more than spots standing out against the grass, just as likely a solitary bush than a native who had stopped in the field to watch them. Still, some of them at least must have been other natives, he thought.

They took a turn around a bunch of thin trees and came upon a child, or at least what Warin assumed was one. They were much shorter than Tyundelorro, almost Warin's height, and was squatting on the side of the road by a stream, watching the water flow by. As the two men and Tyundelorro approached, the young native looked up and started. They stood upright to face the three of them.

"What are those things with you, scavenger?" they asked, the translator using a different, higher-pitched voice for the youth.

"These are new friends from far away," Tyundelorro replied. Warin had noticed that the native had turned their face to the side so as to be understood by the child in front as well as Dav standing next to them. *"They have come to meet us and our families."*

The youth studied the men for a long time, tilting their head to the side. *"Where is their other leg? Are they crippled?"* they asked.

Dav took a small step toward the youth, who focused intently on him as he did. "We only have two legs," he said. "It is the way we are."

"Gibberish," the youth said. *"And you shout strangely."*

Tyundelorro grunted. *"Foolish child. Show respect."* The native gestured down the road. *"Run ahead and tell the village we are coming."*

The youth turned and scampered off, faster than Warin would have thought possible. Their gait was an odd type of gallop, with their back leg pushing off while the front two caught the ground only briefly in turn. Soon enough the young native disappeared beyond a hill ahead.

Tyundelorro turned to Dav. *"They were disrespectful to you,"* they said. *"I ask your forgiveness for the child."*

"Some things are universal," Warin mumbled.

Dav glanced at Warin sideways before turning back to the retty. "We understand," Dav replied, holding his hands up. "We know the child meant nothing."

The native continued. *"But it is good that we came across them. They will do as they were told and tell the village. You both will receive a proper welcome when we arrive."*

Off to the left Warin saw the fenced-off expanse of the rettys' outer fields, their ground dark and as yet unplanted for the season, and he knew they were getting close to the village now. The rettys were also growing more frequent. And closer. They were in the fields, unmistakenly rettys now, often in pairs, stopping in their tasks to stand still and watch them. He glanced up the steep side of a hill on the right and saw a group of several natives looking down on them. He looked back at them after they had passed and watched as they rambled down the hill to the road to join a group of natives that Warin just noticed had started following twenty meters or so behind them.

Warin walked around the front of Tyundelorro and came to stand next to Dav. The two were in a rare break in their continued dialogue as they each contemplated what had just been said. He touched Dav's arm and gestured behind them with his head. "We are starting to draw a crowd."

Dav turned to look over his shoulder. "That's not exactly a surprise," he said. Dav turned back around to draw Tyundelorro's attention to rettys following them.

The native looked, then raised a hand to them well above their head. Many in the crowd did the same. Tyundelorro turned back to Dav. *They are curious about you. They want to see your greeting at Oollaroa. Many would greet you warmly and travel there with us but for the smell of the cart.*

Warin shook his head. "We're going to make a great first impression with the garbage man as our escort."

Dav clamped his hand over his headset's microphone. "Don't be rude," he said sharply to Warin. "Our friend is a very respected member of the village. And they perform an important role."

"So do garbage men," Warin replied.

"They are not the garbage man. They help their food grow to better feed the whole village. It's not the same at all. Anyway, even if they were it wouldn't matter; they don't think of their roles in the village the way you or I would. I keep telling you, they're more utilitarian. You can't just assume the same kind of sociological attitudes that humans have to something."

Warin glanced back at the rettys behind them. "I'm not assuming anything. I'm seeing it."

Dav scowled at Warin and looked away. Warin looked back at the crowd of natives following them. There were at least two dozen of them now, and they ambled behind, making no effort to catch up. They did just look curious to him, not threatening at all. Yet he wasn't sure he could read an alien creature with any certainty.

"Are you sure you know how to do this?" Warin asked Dav. "Meet the villagers, a first-contact situation, open up diplomatic relations, whatever you want to call it? I know it's gone very well with our friend here, but are you sure that's going to be how it goes with the others?"

"I am, yes," Dav replied. "I've watched traders looking to sell their wares enter this village plenty of times. There's a few words and gestures somewhat special for the occasion of asking for permission to enter, but it's simple stuff, barely even qualifies as ceremonial. I have no concerns at all."

"We're not just some traveling craftsmen looking to trade some necklaces, Dav."

"That doesn't matter. If anything we'd probably get some leeway with them on it all as we are so alien. They're not paranoid or suspicious, Warin. They never developed an instinctual fear of outsiders. Not like us."

"What do you mean, 'not like us'?"

"Exactly that. Look." Dav turned to face him. "We evolved from a small primate, right? Our ancestors weren't the strongest or the fastest animal around. Not even close. They were more often food for other animals that were. Prey. Because of that, early on we developed a heightened sense of danger, of fear to survive. Which was a good thing—it kept us in the game while our brains grew larger and we got smarter, craftier. Being wary and suspicious of anything new around you was integral. Even the first modern humans needed it. A lot of the time resources were scarce, and a strange new animal or another tribe showing up on your land could mean starvation if not outright death for you and your family. Fear of the other is deeply ingrained in all of us. It's an instinct. But not the rettys. They evolved differently."

"How?"

Dav gestured to Tyundelorro next to him. "Well, just look at them. They're huge. And strong. There are very few animals on this entire planet that could threaten an adult retty. And a whole family of them, nothing would even try. Their evolutionary path was much easier than ours; instead of scraping by on their wits, in constant fear of attack or death, they just grew too big for anything else to threaten them."

"And without the constant pressure to survive their evolution didn't stagnate?"

"Apparently not. It likely took them much longer to evolve than we did, but turns out getting bigger and stronger than any predators can be a successful path too. One that never depended on the instinct for suspicion and paranoia like we needed. That's my theory, anyway."

"And what does Bela think of your theory? Evolutionary biology is more her area."

Dav frowned, reflecting for a moment, then replied, "She said it was interesting."

The tops of the village popped out from beyond the rise in the road ahead as they reached the flattened plateau that it rested on. The ground on both sides of the road dipped back down again rather steeply past the crest about a meter, even as the road itself stayed at the level of the village ahead, creating a kind of dry moat feature in the area around the village proper. A short, latticed fence of crisscrossing wooden stakes circled the village, only interrupted where it stopped at two thick, squat trees bordering on both sides of the village entrance. Just outside the entrance, the road widened out into a wide and flat area that was filled with rettys, at least twenty of them watching the trio as they approached.

Most of the crowd was disorganized onlookers of various ages and sizes, all of them alternating between glancing at each other and back at the visitors, apparently having dropped what they had been doing to come and see when news of their arrival had reached the village. Warin saw one of the rettys near the left side of the crowd still carried a half-woven basket in their hands.

Two rettys stood in front of the crowd, stoically watching them, unmoving. They both wore dark tunics with a white patterned trim that looked neat and clean. The one on the left was larger, about the same height as Tyundelorro. They appeared young and stood at their full height, holding a staff to the ground to their side like a walking stick. The hair on their arms was bound in tight buns in rows along the back, which sprouted tufts in the center and was dyed deep blue. Around their neck it was woven into braids that looped around like a collar. The one on the right, the slightly smaller one, looked older and more hunched-over, their hair fashioned into loops that hung down both sides of their arms and neck. They rested their head on their hands on top of their staff in front of them.

"The child was right, scavenger. You have made strange new friends," the translator said for one of them in a gravelly voice, which Warin could not tell for certain but thought was for the older one.

"Indeed I have." Tyundelorro dropped the harness from their torso, stepped out of it, and approached the pair. Dav and Warin followed behind.

As Tyundelorro approached the crowd they put out their hands, palms up. The native stopped just before the two in the front, bowed their head deeply, and held for a long time prostrate like that before stepping to the side. They gestured back to Warin and Dav. *"I have brought these new ones to you, who ask permission to enter our village in friendship. This is Dav human human being and Warin human human being."* Tyundelorro turned to gesture at the two natives. *"Friend Dav and friend Warin, this is Edirilla the leader, and the next leader Rawilline."*

Dav stepped forward, putting out his palms facing upward.

Warin copied his action. "We are honored to be in your presence," he said, very solemnly. "Allow us the privilege of entering beyond your gates and calling your home ours as well for a brief time."

Edirilla and Rawilline put out their hands facing upward and nodded at them both in turn. *"The child said you shout,"* the gravelly voice, clearly the older one, said.

"Yes, it is how we are able to speak. We do not have the mastery of the face such as your kind has."

"You can understand but cannot speak as the civilized do?" Rawilline asked, the translator giving them a deep monotone voice. *"Were you ill? Did you lose your ability to speak normally?"*

"No. No illness. Just the way we are." Dav said. He tapped his headset. "This tool helps me understand you and speaks for me in return."

Rawilline stepped closer to Dav. *"Yes,"* they said. *"I see that it shouts for you. You make your own noises, then this turns them into ours. Amazing tool."* They reached out for the headset.

Dav put his hands up to hold it on his head. "I can show it to you if you want," he said. "But you must be careful. Gentle. If it breaks we cannot talk."

Edirilla grunted, and Rawilline turned to face them. *"Leave it,"* they said. *"We can understand them and that is enough."* The younger retty stepped back to stand next to their leader, who looked back at the two visitors. *"What brings strange creatures such as you to our land?"* they asked. *"If you have come to trade our goods are modest."*

"I am sure your village has fine wares that would honor any trade," Dav said. "But we are not here for that. We have come to learn of you and your people. Of your customs and your ways."

"You seek only knowledge?"

"Yes," Dav said, nodding. "It is very valuable to us."

Edirilla's head shook sharply. *"You are scribes."*

"My friend is," Dav said, gesturing back at Warin. "He is a scribe. I am a… student."

"A useful pairing," Edirilla said. *"You learn things and your mate keeps your record."*

"Mate?" Warin said.

Dav turned to him, muting his headset. "You could do worse," he said and turned back to Edirilla. "Yes, he is very helpful to me in my study. We together know the joy of learning."

"It is a noble calling. We are honored by your presence. You are welcome in our village, to learn of us and we of you. You will accompany me back to the public center where we can talk more."

"Of course. Thank you." Dav bowed deeply to the village leader.

Tyundelorro placed their hand on Dav's shoulder to get his attention. *"I must be off, to get these carcasses under a grinding stone,"* they said. *"You have been well received in my home, friend Dav."*

Dav smiled up at the native. "We have, and thank you, friend Tyundelorro, for all your help. I hope you will come find us again when your work is finished today. I will enjoy talking more." Dav held out his hand to the native.

Tyundelorro looked at it. *"The greeting custom?"*

Dav laughed. "It works for parting as well."

Tyundelorro took his hand and shook it, then turned to Warin and shook his as well. *"Such a strange custom,"* they said, and turned back to their cart.

Dav turned to Warin. "See?" he said. "That couldn't have gone any better. Piece of cake."

Warin nodded. "So far so good, at least. Though that Rawilline seemed a little suspicious of us."

"Stop being so paranoid. They were just curious. A fellow inquisitive mind." Dav turned to walk toward Edirilla, who was waiting for them to accompany them. "Come on, honey. Let's not leave our host waiting."

Six

THE PROCESSION INTO the village was impromptu. Much of the crowd from the gate dispersed, but some, older rettys, younger ones, followed the humans at a polite distance, as Edirilla and Rawilline led the two men into the village.

The cobblestone path narrowed just past the gate, as it branched off to the left and right to circle the inside of the fence. Straight ahead appeared to be a main thoroughfare through the center of the village. The native's domed structures lined both sides of it in uneven rows. They were fairly uniform: tan, clay hemispherical structures roughly ten meters in diameter and a little over six meters at their height, with a doorless entryway facing the path underneath a canopy in the modest front yards of scrub and tightly packed earth of each home. Wafts of smoke rose out of the top of many from indoor fires, as he had seen from the observation post, but up close he also saw they had rows of slit windows circling high up their sides, and deep etchings in their surface, ornate swirls and patterns carved into them, some of which were incredibly intricate.

Rettys were out in front of most of the domes, eating, working on crafts or chores, or otherwise socializing in small groups underneath their canopies. They all stopped what they were doing to watch as the humans passed by, often walking up to the edge of their yards to do so, though none of the natives made a move to approach any closer.

Warin looked around at the assembled rettys. He couldn't sense any animosity in them, or fear, or anything that suggested the slightest aggressiveness. Though he knew with an alien he couldn't trust any impression of their demeanor. They all looked at him with that same strange expression of calm curiosity mixed with bemusement that Tyundelorro had had on the hill. They would turn their heads back and forth fluidly, letting each of their eyes focus on him, or blink very deeply, all three eyes in unison, also just as the scavenger had when they had first met them. Warin wondered if it was meant as some kind of greeting, but if it was, Dav's translator didn't register it.

The village was quiet, though not completely silent. Here and there one of the rettys would grunt, or cough, or a distant ring of metal being shaped would ring somewhere far off, or the creak of a wagon wheel a street or two away. There was a hum to the village, as any gathering of many living beings in close proximity would have, the little sounds of their existence blending together into a background buzz, but it was far more muted than a human settlement would be. Warin could hear his shoes on the cobblestones beneath him, even the faint wind whistling by. He found it unnerving. His shoulders tensed and he kept clasping and unclasping his hands.

"Calm down," Dav whispered to him, leaning in to his ear.

Warin nodded sharply and took several deep breaths.

Edirilla led the two men to the center of the village, where the buildings and other structures fell off behind a roughly circular border. At the center of the plaza was a slightly raised platform underneath a large open tent. The crowd of natives that had been following them fell behind, milling about at the edges of the space. Edirilla and Rawilline continued on underneath the canopy toward the platform, where there were benches arranged in two rows with a path up the middle that led to a single bench centered between them.

As Warin was about to follow them underneath it, Dav placed a hand in his way.

"Wait," he said. "There's a certain etiquette to observe here."

Edirilla turned back to face them as they sat down on the front bench, with two legs facing forward and their third stretched out behind. Rawilline took up a position standing to the left of the chief. Edirilla placed their hands out in front of them. *"Please enter and be heard,"* they said.

Dav nodded and stepped in. Warin followed behind.

"Is this like their throne room?" he asked.

Dav shook his head. "No, it's not… You know what? That's close enough."

The two men climbed up onto the tall, retty-sized bench directly in front of Edirilla. "I thank you for welcoming us," Dav said as he turned and sat down, his feet dangling in the air. He cleared his throat and reached out his hands, palms facing up. "I, Dav from faraway lands and here in friendship, humbly accept your audience. May my entreaty benefit the village," he said very formally.

Rawilline shook their head in a circular motion. *"You are considerate to follow our customs,"* they said.

Dav bowed his head. "I am a guest in your village. It is the least I can do."

Rawilline blinked. *"Though that is the greeting of those who come to the chief with pleas of land for a home. Are you a petitioner? Do you wish to build your home in our valley?"*

Dav sat straight in his seat. "No. Not at all," he said quickly. "Your lands are beautiful and bountiful, but they are yours. We have no intention to settle here. We are only visitors. I swear. I apologize if I have erred in my greeting."

Edirilla raised their hand. *"Your greeting was fine, if a bit inexact,"* they said, glancing at Rawilline. *"However, we can make allowances for such strangers to our land as you."*

Rawilline said, bowing slightly. *"I meant no challenge. I merely meant to inform you. You did say you were here to learn of us."*

"And I thank you for the knowledge," Dav said. "I would love to learn of all the greetings and their nuance. That is indeed why we are here. To learn everything we can about you."

"And I would be interested in learning more about you and your kind," Rawilline said.

Dav nodded. "Of course."

"Especially where it is your kind comes from," Rawilline added.

Dav started to stumble for an answer, but Edirilla raised a hand as a young retty entered from the side of the tent, holding a tray in their hands that had a large bowl with a ladle and a stack of lipped plates on it. *"That can wait,"* the chief said as the youth placed the tray on a small table next to Edirilla. They nodded to them and the youth retreated.

Edirilla grabbed the bowl and a plate off the top and dished out a thick substance onto the plate, and handed it to Rawilline. They prepared another one and handed it out to Dav. *"Would you share our midday meal?"* they asked.

Dav took the plate with a nod. "Thank you."

Warin took the next plate from the chief almost without realizing it until it rested on his lap. He looked down at the food. It was a brown, lumpy paste-like substance that glistened with a strange purplish tint where the light reflected off it. It had a somewhat musty odor that in itself wasn't unpleasant as much as it was unfamiliar.

He leaned over to Dav. "What is this?" he whispered.

"Basic grain boiled in water. Like porridge."

"Is it safe to eat?"

"Of course it is," Dav replied. "Why wouldn't it be?"

"Because it's food from a completely different planet with a completely different chemical makeup than the one we come from? Are you sure our systems can even digest it?"

"People on planet have been recreating native meals to try out for years. Nobody has had any problems. At worst you could get a little upset stomach." Dav pulled a clump of it free and plopped it into his mouth. He chewed it vigorously. "It's much better than station food. Fresh. All natural." His eyebrows raised in surprise. "And it has an interesting, almost lime-like aftertaste."

Dav began talking with Edirilla about the food, asking questions about its name, what was in it, how it was prepared, as he continued to eat. The chief was quickly absorbed in the conversation, as they answered Dav in what seemed like pride to Warin. Just as with Tyundelorro on the walk to the village, the conversation began to move about almost aimlessly, from the food to the fabric of the tent, to the origin of the stone necklace around Edirilla's neck. Warin slid away from Dav down the bench, tuning out their talk as he eyed his still-untouched food.

He poked at it with his finger. It jiggled slightly, and felt rubbery, having already started to congeal. Warin had grown up on station food—rations, packets of protein facsimile, processed and freeze-dried, colored and artificially flavored. No different than he had eaten at every outpost he had been stationed on, including this one. That was what he was used to, what he was most at ease with. Now this, natural food, from an alien planet… he didn't think he could do it.

Edirilla and Dav, both having finished their own meals and

set their plates aside, were fully engrossed in conversation and oblivious to him. Rawilline, standing next to their chief, turned to look at Warin. He had no idea how to interpret the way the native was looking at him, and he shifted in his seat under the native's gaze. Rawilline cocked their head to the side, first to the right and then to the left, then looked down at the end of the bench below them on their left. Resting there was the retty's own plate of food, sitting uneaten as well. Rawilline looked back at Warin and shook their head in a circular motion.

Warin placed his plate on the bench next to him and slid it away. He looked back up at Rawilline and nodded with a smile. The native mimicked him, then blinked each of their eyes in succession, left, middle, right.

"It's about time you reported in," Gare said in Warin's earpiece. He could hear the exasperation in her voice.

"Sorry," he replied. "It's been a little busy down here."

Warin had sat and watched the interaction between Dav and the chief for another hour before deciding to slip away, which neither the xenologist nor the native even noticed. He had wandered about the village for a while, under the quiet gaze of the villagers, until he had found this quiet, somewhat isolated spot in a grove of small trees, an orchard of some kind on the far end of the village. He leaned against the border fence, looking up at the mountain where the observation post was. At least generally where it was. He couldn't see much from this distance. Maybe just a thin dark line in the rocks that would be the observation deck windows. Though he was probably just imagining that.

"What's your status? Have you made contact with the rettys?" Gare asked.

"Yes. We're in the village. Dav is with their chief right now."

"How is he doing?"

"He's having the time of his life. When I left him he was getting them to tell him all about their home-building techniques."

"Good. Was there any difficulty?"

"Not with the rettys, no." Warin stretched out his arm, which had started to tighten and feel sore. "There was a little incident before we encountered them, but we got through it."

"An incident?"

"It's nothing serious. Just a little stampede we got caught in."

"A stampede?"

"Yeah. We're both fine. One of the natives helped us out. It's actually how we made first contact."

"Well that's one way to do it, I guess."

"I'll file a report about it later." Warin looked over his shoulder back into the village. Several rettys stood here and there in the trees, grabbing leaves and popping them into their mouths. "Right now I'd draw too much attention working on my pad. It's enough that they see me babbling away to myself like this."

"There are rettys around you right now?"

"Of course. I told you, we're in their village. Everywhere I go there are natives. And they're all looking at me."

"You mean they're following you."

"No, not like that. Well, there's one kid who I think has been around since we got here, but it's not organized or anything. It's purely curiosity." Warin glanced back at the natives again, shaking his head. "I gotta say, their reaction to us has been weird."

"In what way?" Gare asked.

"I don't know. It's just... They're so accepting of us. All of them are, even the young ones. They don't seem wary at all when two aliens just come waltzing into their home. I mean,

I'm not complaining. It's great for us. We don't have to worry about them being aggressive and throwing shit at us or anything. I can't imagine that if one of them came up to a pre-Bronze Age settlement on Earth they'd have been so welcome."

"No, they definitely wouldn't have been," Gare said. "Probably would have been chased into the forest as a demon. And then the forest would have been burned down. But that's the difference between us and them."

"Seems almost naive."

"It's worked for them," Gare said. Warin could almost sense her shrug.

Warin took an oxygen tablet from his pouch and continued. "Anything new going on back at base?"

"The FSS *Ignacio* arrived in system about an hour ago," she replied. "Should be in orbit by late next week to start taking up the staff from the stations on the other continents."

"That was fast," Warin said. "Aren't they a month or so early?"

"Apparently they were in the area," Gare replied. "And there's no point in putting it off. There's nobody left for the staff at those posts to study."

Warin grimaced. "And what about the Bug?"

"Took another five villages since the survey last week. And all the major port settlements on both sides of our valley. The mountains around here seem to be a bit of an impediment to it, so it's been slowed reaching us."

"How long?"

"Hard to tell. I asked Bela for a revised estimate but she's still busy with something else."

Or just ignoring you, Warin thought. "Well, anyway," he said. "We've made contact and Dav is deep into it now, so mission accomplished. I'm feeling kind of sore, so I'll rest here tonight and start back up to base first thing tomorrow."

"I need you to stay with Dav," Gare replied. "Give him backup."

Warin sighed. "He doesn't need it, Gare."

"I still want him to have it."

"There's nothing for me to do down here. I can't even communicate with the locals. Dav is perfectly safe with the rettys by himself. They're not aggressive, remember? I just want to get back up to my job."

"You can work remotely for now," Gare said with the slightest stern tone in her voice. "Just a couple of days, Warin. I still want someone down there with him. If for no other reason than to remind him he needs to check in with me every once in a while."

Warin sighed, rubbing his head. "Just a couple of days?"

"Three. Maybe four," she said, then added quickly, "You're not missing anything up here, Warin. I promise. Just think of it as a vacation. Get some sun. Relax."

"Fine," Warin said glumly. "Though it doesn't feel like as much of a choice as you're making it sound."

"It isn't. Base out."

Warin tapped his earbud to close the link. He should have just outright asked her to sign off on his transfer if he stayed.

He turned around, leaning on the fence, facing back into the orchard. There seemed to be more rettys among the trees than before. Occasionally one of them would gesture to another native with them, and Warin could just barely see their face twitch, or eyes blink, and know they were saying something. Most likely about him. Sometimes they would turn themselves away from him as they did so, perhaps not fully confident that Warin couldn't understand them.

He sighed. The rettys' passive type of attention was off-putting. Better than fear, sure, or manic excitement, but the casual watching from a distance made him feel like an oddity, a freak of some kind. And not a particularly interesting one. But then again, that was kind of what he was here. One of only two like him that had ever stepped foot in the village that any of the rettys had ever seen. The funny-looking thing, short and olive-skinned, with very little hair that had nothing fancy done with it at all. Such a plain-looking creature. And with only two legs! However was he able to stay upright? He half-thought them staring at him in fear would be better.

A few fenceposts to his right Warin saw a young retty—very young, he guessed, as they were shorter than he was, clumsily trying to reach a low-hanging branch by balancing themself off the top of the fence rail on two legs, with the third snaked through underneath. They leaned toward a nearby tree, stretching out their arms. But the branches were just out of their reach. The youth stretched even farther out, putting themself in an even more unstable position. The fence rail started to creak under their weight.

Warin walked over to the tree the young native was leaning toward. The branch they were reaching for was slim, shooting off a thicker one near the trunk. To Warin's eye it looked pliable.

He stepped up the trunk of the tree and, by lifting himself up just a little more by grabbing at the base of another branch, managed to reach it. He bent the branch downward to the youth, careful not to break it off in his hands. The young retty snatched and came away with a pair of leaves. They jumped down off the fence to the ground, looking at their prize.

Warin stepped down and stood in front of the youth. They looked up at Warin, their face twitching, eyes blinking.

"I'm sorry, I don't understand," Warin said just as fruitlessly to them. He waved his hand in front of his own eyes back and forth slowly. "Blind. Numb face."

The youth blinked deeply and shook their head back and forth a few times. Warin didn't know if they were still speaking or if he had confused them. They put one of the leaves in their mouth and chewed it slowly. After a moment they reached out their hand to Warin, offering the other leaf to him.

Warin shook his head, smiling. "No, that's okay. You can have them both. I won't tell."

The youth seemed to understand, as they withdrew their hand, pressing the leaf close to its torso. They blinked at Warin deeply and bounded off past him. Warin turned to watch them disappear in the trees. Two adult natives nearby watched as the youth passed and then turned back to Warin and put out their hands, palms facing upward to him. Warin nodded and did the same.

A few days. Maybe four, he thought. After that, he'd leave Dav down here and go back to the base, no matter what Gare did about his transfer.

Seven

A FLY HAD gotten into the tent, and Warin swatted at it absently as he studied his pad. He had his account profile up and opened to the history tab. He scratched the back of his head and breathed deeply. There were all the actions he had taken that morning. As well as yesterday on the reports Rek had filed. And there was his work from the night before last, his report about his and Dav's first contact. But it ended there. His account work history was blank before that. And he hadn't cleared it.

"Goddammit, Lil," he muttered to himself. He opened a comm window on the pad and tapped Lil's name. But it only chimed once before he closed the window abruptly, folded up his pad, and put it back in his pack by the foot of his sleeping bag. Such a stupid thing for her to do. And such a sloppy job covering it up.

But whatever. He'd deal with it later.

He slipped on a fresh pair of shorts and shirt, put his earpiece in, and grabbed his belt and empty canteen in one hand as the other unzipped the opening to his tent. He crawled out and got to his feet with a deep stretch. It was already late in the morning and the sun was about halfway to its zenith. It flashed at him from between the orchard tree leaves above him. He glanced around as he snapped his belt in place, checking with his hands that his holster and other odds and ends attached to it were secure. The most he saw was a native ten or twelve rows off to his right, half unseen through the foliage between them. He'd noticed that among the rettys, eating the leaves was more of a late afternoon/evening activity, perhaps as some sort of dessert—or perhaps a recreational activity left for after the end of the day's work. So there never were many natives in the grove this early. And beyond that, the trees in this part of the grove were taller, older, their color somewhat muted, and he guessed from how the rettys didn't pluck at their leaves or even come near them as much, not as appetizing. It made the spot isolated enough for privacy, yet with a common path just four rows to his left not so far away from everything to make it a slog to get anywhere.

Since their arrival, Dav had completely immersed himself in the village and among the rettys, and had been staying in Edirilla's home as an honored guest. That was a little too much exposure for Warin—he was more than happy with his little private campsite in the grove. Dav still checked in with him in the evenings. He'd excitedly try and tell Warin all about what he had talked about with the chief and other natives all day. Their farming habits, their folklore, rudimentary scientific concepts they had already come to. Warin listened to the xenologist, but didn't retain much; it all came out in a jumble of random tidbits and trivia, a collection of excitedly recounted factoids that often had no connection to each other. Dav was like a kid in a candy shop grabbing sweets. He wasn't sure how he would ever be able to make everything he was learning into something resembling an organized report.

Warin exited the grove and walked toward the village center, the dirt path under his feet slowly turning back into smooth cobblestone. The suns bore down hard on him as he got out from the shade of the trees. Almost immediately he felt the sweat on his forehead and arms start to collect. He grabbed an oxygen tablet and popped it into his mouth.

The domes in this part of the village were slightly smaller than they were along the main path into town, with a steeper angle in the dome and less complex etchings, though some exhibited colored highlights in their lines of blue and red. Natives sat outside every one of them on log stools or short benches at tables, carving, weaving a basket, cleaning linens, or just talking. It seemed the common practice of the rettys to spend most of their time outside in their doorways, usually underneath the canopy for shade. Warin assumed the only things they ever did inside were prepare meals (which of course they'd bring outside to eat), sleep, bathe, and probably procreate. However that was done. It gave the surroundings a very social, alive feeling, as the natives would interact with their neighbors to both sides and across the paths from them, as well as with passers-by. And of course every one of them would look up at him and stare as he approached. He would nod at them as they passed by, a gesture many of them would return.

There were four or five wells made of stone and wood spread out in the village. Beyond being the primary source of water for the natives living nearby, the wells were more of a gathering place, somewhere the natives would stand in groups or sit on one of the random log stools about the open area as they silently conversed with each other, sipping from cups or nibbling on snacks.

Warin had become a common sight at the well over the last few days, and many of the natives turned from their groups to face him and greeted him both with his human nod and the native outstretched hands. Warin returned the double greeting to them with a smile as he walked right up to the well. Nobody was in line to draw water at this time of the day. He had learned quickly to wait till later to stop by to avoid the crowd of natives getting what they needed in the early morning.

Warin rested his canteen against the side of the well. He undid the rope and held it loosely as he dropped the conical bucket over the side, where he heard it splash a second or two later. He could feel the bucket get heavier on the rope quickly as it started to sink into the water below. When he thought he had enough, he pulled the bucket back up and tied the rope off. He tipped the hanging bucket to the side and ran the water on his hand, cupping it to his mouth. The water was crisp and cold, so much so that it made his teeth sting a little. He took another handful and splashed it on his face and the back of his neck, rubbing it in until his skin was near dry again. He lifted his shirt and splashed more handfuls on his chest and under his arms, enjoying the mild shock of the cold water on his torso. Finally, he picked up his canteen and held it under the bucket as he tipped it over, cascading the water down, filling it haphazardly.

Warin turned as he let go of the bucket to see an old retty standing nearby, watching him. Very old, Warin thought. They leaned very heavily on a staff in both their hands, their body slumped over so much their height looked nearly halved, their head at eye level with Warin. Their body hair was barely more than brittle-looking single strands here and there, not enough to braid or fashion. Deep lines ran along their face and shoulders, down across the muscles on their thin arms that were soft, even under the clear exertion of carrying so much of their weight through them onto the point of the staff.

Warin slung his canteen across his shoulders and stood upright, facing the old native. He noticed his still-moist shirt had ridden up along his right side, and he pulled it down with a sheepish grin. The retty didn't move. He looked closer at their eyes and saw the milky film that covered them. The old native must be half-blind, he thought.

Warin put out his palms facing out toward them. The native nodded to him in return, but did not otherwise move. They stood looking at each other for a long moment, which made Warin fidget in place.

"Hello," Warin said to the native, if for no other reason than to break the silence.

The old retty shook their head slightly, then spoke, "Ehhh-oo-hhh."

Warin smiled. "That's close. Very close," he said. "Hello," he said again, more slowly, stressing both syllables.

The native tried again. "Hehh-oohh."

"Hello."

"Heh-loohh."

Warin nodded at the retty. "You got it. Hello." Warin tapped his chest several times. "My name is Warin. Warin."

The old retty leaned their head in, turning it side to side, focusing each of their eyes on Warin in turn.

"Warin," he repeated, tapping his chest.

"Wah-rin," the retty said very slowly, carefully. Warin nodded to them and the native repeated it more confidently, pointing at him. "Wahrin."

"Exactly," Warin said. He jabbed his finger into his chest, saying "Warin." He pointed at the native. "You?"

The old retty shook their whole body and neck like a horse and looked at Warin. "Ollahnah," they said.

"Ollahnah," Warin repeated. "Your name is Ollahnah."

"Eck-at-eee," the native said.

"Eck-at-eee? What… Oh, right! Exactly!" Warin laughed. "It's nice to meet you," he said. "Nice to get to talk to someone."

The old retty and Warin stood there looking at each other in silence, long enough that Warin started to feel awkward. Over the last few days he had started to get a grasp on reading the demeanor of the rettys, to pick up on some of their body language. Or at least he thought he had. He was pretty sure it wasn't all that different from humans, especially in the general. And looking at this old native standing in front of him, he got the distinct impression that they were waiting on him.

Warin took his canteen off from across his shoulder and unscrewed the cap. "Right. Let's try more." He poured a tiny amount of water out into his cupped hand and held it out to Ollahnah. The old native leaned forward to look more closely. "Water," Warin said. "Water." He brought his hand up to his mouth. "Drink water." Warin slurped up the water into his mouth. "Understand?" He poured more water into his hand. "Water."

The old native reached out and poked a finger into the puddle in Warin's hand. "Wah-ter."

"Eck-at-eee!" Warin said. He pointed back and forth between the water and Ollahnah. "What do you call this?" he asked. "What do you call water?"

Ollahnah followed Warin's finger back and forth, then seemed to understand. "Esh," they said.

"Esh? You call it esh?"

"Eck-at-eee," Ollahnah said.

"All right," Warin said. "Basic substance, very simple word. Makes sense." He brought the water to his mouth again. "And this? What is drink? Drink?" Ollahnah stared at him blankly. "Drink? What do you call drinking? Drink esh?"

Ollahnah followed Warin's hand as it went back and forth to his mouth, tilting their head left to right a few times. "Ell," they said.

"To drink is ell?" Warin asked. He drank from his hand. "Ell esh?"

The old retty stared at Warin in a way he took to be confusion. They sort of grunted at him and held out their hand, cupping it similar to the way Warin had. Warin took a step forward and tipped his canteen to spill water into Ollahanh's hand, doing it slowly in case he had misunderstood. Ollahnah's hand filled with water. They held it up to Warin's face, little drips coming out from between their fingers. "Esh," they said loudly. "Esh." The old native brought their hand up to their mouth. "Ell," they said and drank. After a few sips, they brought their hand back to Warin. "Esh," they said again, opening their hand and letting the remaining few drops fall to the ground.

Warin furrowed his brow. "Okay, give me a second here," he mumbled. He poured more water into his hand. "So, when it's in my hand, or I guess in the well, or in a river or something, it's esh." He brought his hand up to his mouth. "But when I go to drink it, it's called ell. What you call water changes with… what you do with it? What it's doing?" He held his hand out again. "Esh," he said, then brought his hand back to his mouth. "Ell."

Ollahnah rose up. "Eck-at-eee!" they almost yelled. They placed a hand gently on Warin's shoulder. "Wahrin," they said. "Joolid."

"Joolid," Warin said almost under his breath as he looked at the large hand on him. "I'm going to assume that means friend." Warin turned back to the old native. "Ollahnah. Joolid."

Ollahnah nodded at him and said, "Eck-at-eee."

A LOT OF the retty vocal language seemed to be like water, the word that described a thing changing depending on its circumstance, what it was being used for, or what you did with it. At least as far as Warin could figure out. He was not a linguist, and his focus was split between trying to teach Ollahnah just as much as he was trying to learn from them. So for the most part he focused on basic words with the old native, and just moved on whenever it started to get into complex usage. Full sentences or any kind of meaningful communication would have to wait. He still got a few basic things—*urk* was dirt, *nhahht* was the sky, with clouds being *oohl,* the mountains were *urlattin,* and the well was *urbaw,* though he wasn't certain that wasn't just the stone of the well and not the well itself.

He sat with Ollahnah by the well for about an hour, until a younger retty came to collect them. Ollahnah did not seem pleased about it, as they pushed off the gentle hands the young native put on their arm, vocalizing with them too quickly for Warin to follow, even though Warin suspected Ollahnah was communicating verbally to the young retty instead of visually for his benefit. But soon enough Ollahnah acquiesced, and allowed the retty to lead them away from the well.

As the old native left, they turned to face Warin. "Wahrin. Joolid," they said.

Warin nodded. "Ollahnah. Joolid."

Warin watched the young retty escort Ollahnah away, feeling somewhat exhilarated. The old native was the first retty to try and talk to him. At least in a way he could understand. Sometimes he felt the others had tried, but the way they talked, visually. They'd stare at him for a while, and he could see some of it, but not enough to even begin to understand. Eventually they'd give up and walk away. They didn't grasp or just didn't believe that his vision wasn't good enough.

But Ollahnah had. Probably because of their own bad vision did they realize his problem, because they too couldn't see well enough to read microexpressions. And so they tried verbally with him. Shouting. And it had worked. For the first time in days, Warin felt he had accomplished something. Just a handful of words, nowhere close to being able to really talk with any of the rettys, but still, it was something.

Instead of heading back to his tent to hide like he had done every other day, Warin wandered about aimlessly for the rest of the afternoon, stopping occasionally to watch the rettys at various tasks. He'd stand apart as they worked stone, chipping and smoothing them into tools or ornaments, spun flax into string on basic spindles, or ground grain down in large basins with smooth rocks. He tried on a few occasions to engage with them, trying out a few of the words that he had learned. Which itself was awkward, as he hadn't realized until he first tried that he had never learned a word for greeting. It never amounted to much; they'd look up at him and reply, but visually at first, to which all he could think to do was repeat himself or stare dumbly back. Some of the natives he tried with would get the idea and would say things verbally to him, and he managed to pick up a few more words that way (*ohhmilla* were what they called their homes, *urkhett* were carving stones, or maybe just the particular granite one the retty he talked to was working with, *emp* were the log stools everyone sat on), but they would not be interested in teaching him more and would soon go back to their work. He'd move on soon enough, leaving them alone.

In the late afternoon, he was sitting on a long log at another of the village wells to rest his feet when his earbud toned. *"Call from Lil,"* it said.

Warin sighed and tapped the earbud. "Open," he said.

Lil's voice was sharp in his ear. "Hey, you tried to call earlier?"

"Yeah, I did," he said.

"What's up? How's the village?"

"It's fine. Very relaxed. Kind of like a historical tour."

"I bet. Gare's given the go-ahead for the rest of us to visit. We're planning to come down in a few days. Anything we should bring special?"

"Toilet paper." Warin got up from the log and turned until he faced away from all the natives standing nearby. "Listen, this morning I was working on my pad and noticed my auto-fills had been deleted. Nothing major, just some application data I use every time I file a report."

"Okay."

"When I looked at my account, I found that my keystroke history had been wiped too. All records of my work except for what I'd done in the last couple of days while down here."

"So you're telling me because you think some kind of glitch in the system wiped out all your metadata. Something I need to look at, right?"

"You could look at it, sure." Warin closed his eyes and took a deep breath. "But it sounds more like someone accessed my account, did whatever they did, and then deleted all my metadata after they were done to cover their tracks."

There was a long pause. Then Lil asked, "And why exactly would anyone hack your account?"

"Because I have access to all the filed reports on the rettys? And someone was planning on leaking them to the net servers before they had Ministry approval, to, I dunno, maybe try and spark a protest?"

"Sounds pretty devious," Lil said. "Who do you think it was? Bela?"

"Lil, come on. This is serious. You know my account has access to way more than just the field reports. There's a lot of dangerous information in the database. Weapon schematics. Classified reports."

"What do I care about any of that?"

"You don't, but the Ministry won't make that distinction. Whether it was the access codes for the Mindauri arsenal or the Secretary-General's oatmeal cookie recipe, all they'll see is a security breach and come down like a ton of bricks about it. On whoever did it."

"You should make sure to report it to Gare, then," Lil said.

"I will be," Warin replied tersely. "And whoever it is who might be looking to send Ministry files to a public server might want to think twice about it. Drop the whole pointless idea."

"So preventing a mass extinction is pointless now?" Warin heard a slight crack in her voice.

Warin closed his eyes, pinching the bridge of his nose. "You're not going to be preventing anything, Lil. It's already too late."

"Who said it was too late?"

"Everyone. The data. The Bug is everywhere."

"It's not in this valley," Lil said. "It can't get past the mountains."

"That's only temporary."

"Is it?" Lil snorted. "The bug was supposed to be here by now. That's what all the projections said. But it isn't, is it? It's blocked. So the projections were wrong. Maybe they were wrong about other things. Maybe it will never get through the valley. It's not impossible."

"Have you talked to Bela about this? What does she say?"

"I don't need to ask her what *I* think. I can look at the data too."

"But you're not—" Warin stopped, feeling it was useless. "Fine, do whatever you want, Lil. It's your neck. Just don't go using my account to do it next time."

Lil sighed deeply on the other end. "Warin, I maintain this entire post. The machinery, the power generators, the workstations. The local network servers. Everything. I don't need to hack you to get at files. But even if for some stupid reason I wanted to download the entire Ministry database through your account, I could do it with my eyes closed. And when I was done, you wouldn't have the slightest clue I had."

The channel closed with a sharp click in Warin's ear.

Warin shook his head. She was going to get caught. Lose her commission. Even worse. How much worse depended on how badly she embarrassed the Ministry. And all for a hopeless cause.

He looked up at the mountains in the distance, turning slowly as his eyes moved from one snowy peak to the next all the way around the valley. It was a pretty complete barrier. From what he remembered of the geography, the best path out of the valley was a narrow passage to the north, probably not even as wide as the road outside the village. He assumed there were mountain trails as well in all directions too, ones known to the rettys that they didn't have in their charts, but they were likely rough and inhospitable, possibly not passable by anything most of the year.

He tapped his earbud. "Call Bela."

"Connecting." He stood waiting for a long time to hear her voice, but instead of Bela he got the earbud: "Connection denied."

He went to tap his earbud again, but stopped and stared at the ground. She must still be pissed with him. He ran his foot in a small patch of sand on the ground. He had never thought she was the type to hold grudges. Or that he mattered enough to her to evoke one. But maybe this time was different. All this mattered more to her. He shrugged. Or maybe she was just busy. She could get that way about things, be very obsessive about her work. To the point where she could go days without responding to her communications. Without talking to any-one, even if they were standing right next to her. The dispas-sionate scientist with a tunnel-vision focus. She was almost a cliche.

A group of retty children ran by, and he jumped as they passed. One of them twirled back to face him and let out a high-pitched squeal, and then turned back and kept going, all without missing a step. They continued on past a couple sitting outside their home (their *ohhmilla*) as they ate, hud-dled together over a plate of grain affectionately. One of them flicked grains of their food at the last child to run past.

The idea that the valley was an impenetrable barrier to all that went on in the outside world was very appealing to him.

Eight

He stayed up late waiting for Dav to contact him as he had done the previous nights, but the xenologist never checked in. Warin didn't think much of it other than as a mild annoyance as he turned out his light and crawled onto his air mattress. By the time he awoke, the morning was already nearly gone. He sat up with a yawn and grabbed his pad. There wasn't anything new in his inbox, so the loss of a morning didn't seem to have mattered.

After he ate a food bar and dressed, he unzipped his tent and stuck his head out, looking up through the branches. Both suns were moving across the sky in and out of the intermittent cloud cover above. The ground smelled fresh and he saw tiny droplets in the grass by his head. It must have rained last night and through the morning.

He heard a deep sniffling sound and turned his head at it. Behind him and just inside his little clearing was a retty, crouching against a tree and watching him. Warin looked up at them. Their face met his with the calm, passive expression he had grown used to seeing in the natives. It took him a moment but he recognized them, more from their hairstyle and dark tunic than by their face.

"Rawilline," Warin said as he crawled out of his tent and stood to face them.

The native nodded. "Wahrin," they replied. "Hehllo."

"Hello." Warin smiled. "I see Dav has been teaching you some words." Warin looked around the campsite. "I hope you haven't been waiting long." Rawilline didn't react. Warin continued. "I'd offer you breakfast, but I don't think you'd be able to digest it. Protein bars. Meat-based facsimile."

Rawilline blinked deeply but otherwise was still.

Warin looked around the trees, down at his tent awkwardly. He looked back up at Rawilline, who stared back at him. He couldn't be certain, but he didn't think they were trying to speak visually.

"Is there something I can do for you?" Warin asked, speaking very slowly and deliberately. Immediately he felt foolish doing so. No way Dav could have taught Rawilline enough for them to understand any of that in just a couple of days no matter how carefully he spoke.

Rawilline nodded slowly to Warin, grunting. The native reached into a pocket on their tunic and pulled out something, and extended it across to Warin.

It was Dav's translator headset.

Warin tapped his earbud. "Call Dav."

"Connecting." Warin remained calm as he waited, glancing back and forth between the headset and the native's face. Rawilline still looked calm, betraying nothing. "Connection timed out."

"Retry," he said. He started to feel anxious at Dav's non-answer. And felt it more after a few moments when there was again no connection.

Rawilline extended the headset out further toward him. "Wahrin," they said. "We tahk."

Warin reached out and took the headset from the native with two fingers, and then moved back a step as he put it on. He folded out the glass in front of his right eye. The screen immediately came to life, superimposing Rawilline with a light outline.

He cleared his throat and adjusted the microphone. "Can you understand me?" he asked very slowly.

Rawilline shook their head in a wide arc. Their outline flashed as Warin heard through the headset, *"Yes, friend Warin, you are understood."*

Warin breathed deeply. "Where is Dav?"

"Friend Dav is with Edirilla still. They are teaching each other."

Warin pointed to the headset. "Without this?"

Rawilline did what Warin thought looked like a shrug. *"He said he wanted to learn to shout without the tool so you could use it."* The native flipped their head back. *"He. Strange idea. This... gender thing Dav has told us of. Are there really two kinds of human human being?"*

"It's a little more complicated than that, but let's just say yes for now." Warin took a step closer. "But Dav, he's all right? He's safe?"

"Yes. Friend Dav is safe." The native glanced down at Warin's hand. *"As is friend Warin."*

Warin followed the native eyes down to his own hand. It was wrapped around the grip of his pistol, still holstered on his free-swinging belt. He hadn't realized he had done that. He thought Dav had said they likely wouldn't even know what it was anyway. Seems he had been wrong.

He let go of the gun and slipped the belt on. "It's nothing. Just for protection."

"Are you not safe in our home?"

"Of course I am. I didn't mean..." Warin stopped. He glanced down at the pistol on his belt, shaking his head, and then unclipped the holster from his belt and tossed it back into his tent. "You're right. I have no need for it here. I should not be carrying it. I apologize."

"You have caused no offense," Rawilline said. *"And you should do as you need to. I must ask your forgiveness for alarming you."*

"I wasn't alarmed. It's fine."

"Friend Warin, your face betrays you."

Warin blinked hard. "You can read my face?"

"Some. It is different than ours. But I have watched friend Dav very closely, and I have seen basic words there. Your faces aren't as numb as you think."

Warin suddenly felt self-conscious but pushed it down. "Well, either way," he said, staring at his feet. "It's all right. I thank you for bringing this to me."

"Not at all, friend Warin. I hope you find good use for it. I imagine it will help you feel less isolated in our home."

"Your people have made me feel very welcome," Warin said quickly. "I've picked up a few, ah, shouting words too."

Rawilline nodded. *"That is good. But teaching friend Dav is slow going. He can only shout a few words as of yet, basic statements. And that is with the help of the speaking tool. I would assume without it your progress has been even slower."*

Warin nodded. "It has. This will certainly help." Or skip the need to and just let me talk to them, he thought.

"I am glad, friend Warin." Rawilline took a step back. *"I must go, as I have many tasks for the day. But I would like to return after the suns set to talk with you more, if you permit it."*

Warin nodded quickly. "Of course. I look forward to it."

Rawilline nodded in return, turned, and walked away.

Warin tapped his earbud so hard it made his ear sting for a moment. "Call Dav." But the xenologist still did not answer. Warin silently mouthed several curse words to himself. He tapped his ear again. "Message Dav," he said. After a moment, his earbud beeped and he continued. "Dav, I just got the headset from Rawilline. Thank you, but it would have been real nice for you to give me a heads-up yourself so I don't worry that something happened to you and make me look like a paranoid idiot. Oh, and in case you haven't noticed yet, Rawilline is learning to read your microexpressions. I assume the others you are spending time with are too. So I hope you're being careful about what you say." He tapped his earbud one more time to end the recording.

Warin turned away from his campsite. Over by the trail, he could just barely see the back of Rawilline through the trees as the native kept walking. That native was clever. Warin shook his head. No, there was no need to be patronizing. Rawilline was a very intelligent being, perceptive, calmly thoughtful. The questions they asked, the comments they made, they all felt carefully weighted for the maximum benefit. But they weren't suspicious, there was no tinge of fear or apprehension. Not that he would necessarily know the signs of any of that in an alien. But he just didn't feel it. He laughed to himself. Their conversation later would be interesting.

Warin stared absently at the tree branches above him, breathing very deliberately. He was sure Dav knew that Rawilline could read him already. It wasn't the kind of thing that would escape him. Taking a minute away from his research to keep Warin in the loop about what he was doing, though, *that* would slip his mind. But not the rettys' reading his face. Not that it likely mattered. If the chief or any of the natives asked Dav about hyperspace engines or superstring theory, he'd probably do his best to explain it to them. There likely wasn't anything that they could ask him about that he would not answer.

Well, one thing. Warin hoped.

WARIN DIDN'T SEE Ollahnah anywhere when he got to the well. He felt disappointed at that; he liked the idea of the old retty being the first native he approached to talk to. Instead, the distinction fell on a group of three older rettys who stood nearby talking, ones that Warin had seen at the well each time he visited.

He approached them slowly, and they turned to face him. The monocle glass in front of his right eye showed a faint outline over each of them.

Warin cleared his throat. "Hello," he said tentatively. "Have any of you seen Ollahnah today?"

When the speaker on the headset translated his words, the three natives reared back slightly at the sound. They turned to look at each other. When they turned back to him, the outline around the shorter of the trio flashed. *"You can speak,"* he heard in a soft baritone in his ear.

"Yes," Warin said. "I can now."

"How is this possible?" the short one asked. *"We thought you were dumb."*

The outline of the native on his left flashed as he leaned in toward Warin. *"You have the shouting headband from your mate,"* Warin heard in a gruffer voice in his ear. *"I have heard of this tool. I did not think it real."*

Warin turned and nodded at them. "It is. My friend wants to learn to, ah, shout with your kind without it. So he gave it to me."

"Most generous," the native in the middle said. They rested their hands on the other two's arms. *"I am Undallin. These are my siblings, Morassa and Rellinak."*

Warin smiled at them. "It's good to meet you. I'm Warin."

"Well met, friend Warin," Undallin said. All three of them held out their hands, palms facing up. Warin mimicked the gesture.

"Such an interesting tool that shouts for you," Rellinak said, gesturing toward the headset. *"How does it work?"*

"It's, um, kind of complicated. But basically it watches you when you speak"—Warin tapped the headset speaker on his ear—"and then shouts to me in my words what you say in here. And then this"—he gestured to the microphone—"listens to what I shout and then shouts to you in your words so you understand it."

The three natives leaned in and stared at the headset, and Warin stood still to let them, only placing a hand over the band of it to prevent them from taking it off his head. He noticed behind the trio a small crowd had started to gather, as other rettys watched intently.

Undallin shook their head animatedly. *"Magic,"* they said.

Warin turned to them. "Not magic, no. Just very complex. Advanced."

"Do you have one of these for Ollahnah?" Morassa asked. *"Is that why you wish to see them?"*

"It would be a wonderful gift," Undallin said. *"They are going blind in their age and cannot understand very well. The young don't care for shouting questions to them and don't heed the old one as much as they should. This tool would help Ollahnah greatly."*

"Unfortunately this one would not work for Ollahnah," Warin said. Then he added quickly, "But that doesn't mean we couldn't make another that would."

Undallin bobbed their head. *"That would be a great kindness."*

Warin returned to his original question. "But none of you have seen Ollahnah today?"

A large, muscular retty standing just behind Morassa grunted loudly for attention. *"They are minding the children as they seed Innula field."* They shifted a large scythe-looking tool from their left to right hands. *"They will be there all day."*

Warin turned to the large native. "Innula field? Where is that?"

They pointed over Warin's head to the east, *"Past Ullemuck and Aaan,"* they said. *"By the edge of the forest. I am going back there after I visit my home for a meal. I can take you."*

"I wouldn't want to keep you from your lunch. Your meal."

The large retty shook their head. *"You would honor me with your presence. My mate and child as well."*

Warin started to say something but stopped. He nodded to the large retty. "I would appreciate it. Thank you."

Warin said his goodbyes to the three siblings and followed the large native who he learned was named Frellanda, away from the well.

The retty was particularly chatty as they walked, and in no particular rush as they recounted to Warin the names and anecdotes of the various natives they passed by, stopping to speak with a few and introducing them to Warin with great pomp. Perhaps Frellanda was overdoing it, but Warin played along. Clearly, there was a certain amount of pride to be taken from his company. And the large native was welcome to it if they wanted it.

The village felt like a different place entirely now that he had the translator. The rettys were naturally friendly to him, as they always had been, but now he could interact with them, stop and talk with them as Frellanda introduced him. The questions the retty would ask him were repetitive, sometimes banal, or on things Warin had no idea about, but they were welcome after days of only occasional and very brief talks with Dav. Even the natives' greetings to him as he passed by, ones that without the headset he never would have known of, made him feel less isolated.

Frellanda's home was on the edge of a cluster of domes in no way remarkable from the others in the area. Outside the entrance, a retty nearly as large as Frellanda sat working a grinding wheel on a green stone in their hands. As the two of them approached they looked up. *"Who have you brought with you, mate?"* they asked.

Frellanda walked up and embraced the native, rubbing the top of their head affectionately. They turned to the side and gestured back toward Warin. *"This is Warin, one of the strangers who have come to our village,"* they said. *"I am showing them the fields after my meal."* Frellanda turned back to their mate, *"Friend Warin, this is Yerranha, my mate."*

Warin smiled and nodded. "Hello."

Yerranha held out their hands. *"You are welcome in our home, friend Warin. You will eat with us."*

Warin shook his head. "Thank you, no, that's all right."

"You must have something," Frellanda said. *"You look so thin."*

Warin smirked. "It's the way we are," he said.

Yerranha blinked deeply. *"Bring our guest a small plate,"* they said to Frellanda. *"And see if the child is awake."* Frellanda nodded and entered the dome.

"I'm fine, really, you don't have to," Warin insisted. "I ate this morning."

"You are our guest. It would be wrong to give you nothing," Yerranha replied.

Warin looked at the green stone that Yerranha still had in their hand. "What is it that you are making?" he asked.

The native glanced down at their hand. *"It's nothing. A bauble for the child."* Yerranha held it out to Warin. He took the carved stone and turned it over in his hand.

It was a small figurine of a retty sculpted in a very milky jade stone. The figure stood tall, their neck fully extended, with their arms out at their sides and holding a staff in front and across them. The hair from their neck and arms flowed unbraided and wild like fire, as if in a strong wind, and their tunic draped down low over their feet. Though it might have been more unfinished than an older style of dress. Much of it was still rough, with more detail cut into the head and neck than in the feet.

"Very nice," Warin said, handing it back.

"It's our founder, Tulla, as they jumped from the mountains to land in the spot where our home was built."

"Founder. You mean of this village."

"Yes. Tulla was the leader of the six who built the first home and planted the first field. We are all descended from them. Have you not learned our history?"

"I haven't really been able to till now," Warin replied. "So you worship them."

Yerranha twitched slightly. *"Worship? The founders were wise, and they found this rich land for us, but they are not the land. That provides. We do not worship the founders. We remember them and praise them for the good fortune of the prosperous land that they found for us."*

Frellanda returned, carrying a tray in one hand with three wooden plates with deep rims. In their other hand was a very small child, an infant, who squirmed under Frellanda's forearm, looking around squinting in the sunlight. Their skin looked flushed and soft, and lacked any of the hair of their parents. When Frellanda sat down next to their mate, the child turned their head toward Warin and let out a squeak.

"Insufficient data," the translator said in his ear.

Frellanda set the tray down on the ground between the three of them and grabbed one of the plates, which was full of a grainy purple meal. They handed it across to Warin.

Warin put up a hand. "No, really, it's nice of you to offer, but I'm fine."

"Guests in our home are fed," Yerranha said emphatically. *"Please, friend Warin."*

Warin stared at the plate for a moment, then shrugged. "All right," he said, taking it. "Thank you."

The meal on the plate was dry, and granular, mostly a collection of clumps the size of Warin's thumb. He picked up a kernel and looked at it. It had no discernible smell that he could detect. It was made of black seeds and oval nuts stuck together haphazardly within a flat circular grain. Besides its color it reminded him of homemade granola he had seen once as a child.

With a glance at his hosts, he popped it in his mouth, and let it sit in the center of his tongue. It started to dissolve there almost immediately in his saliva with an odd wooden taste. He moved it around in his mouth and the taste spread. Warin couldn't think of having ever tasted anything like it before. Hickory seasoning was the only thing he could think of as even mildly similar to it. But it was not unpleasant. Just different. He bit down on the kernel and it crunched in his teeth in a satisfying way. He grabbed two or three other kernels from his plate and put them in his mouth.

"It's good," he said to them with a smile.

Yerranha shook her head. *"I am glad it is to your liking, friend Warin. It is a very simple meal. If I had known you would be coming, I could have prepared something special."*

"Oh, I wouldn't have wanted to put you out," Warin said. "This is very good."

The three of them ate from their plates, Frellanda placing his on one knee and sitting the child down on the other. The child squeaked again as they reached out for the large native's hands as Frellanda lifted a scoopful of meal to their mouth.

"You have a beautiful child," Warin said. "How old are they?"

Frellanda looked down at their child and rubbed the top of their head. *"I birthed this little one just before planting started,"* they answered. Frellanda took a kernel of meal and held it out to the child to nibble on. The child nearly disappeared behind the native's large hand.

"They're so small," Warin said.

"We all are once," Frellanda said. Yerranha reached out and stroked the child's head. They glanced over from the meal at their other parent and let out another squeak before going back to the food. *"But they will grow to be big and strong. Already they are large for their age."*

"Next season this little one will go with you for the planting," Yerranha said to their mate. *"And someday, they will pick up your soilturn for you when you grow tired."*

Frellanda grunted three times in succession. A laugh? *"I will be proud on such a day. My child in the fields by my side. But we are many seasons from that."*

Warin said nothing, scooping a mouthful of the grain into his mouth to hide his face behind his hand. The child glanced at him over Frellanda's hand. They blinked at him deeply.

Nine

AFTER LUNCH FRELLANDA led Warin to the fields at a slightly more brisk pace than before, and kept their interaction with other villagers they encountered on the way brief. It made Warin suspect that the native had dallied too long at home and was now late back to work. They kept up a constant conversation with Warin as they walked, though. Warin let them do most of the talking, as he had to jog lightly to keep pace with the large native's stride.

"Inulla is a new field, only a few seasons old now," they said. *"It is still very rocky and the soil is not very rich yet. In a few more seasons it will be better, but even so, it gets seed and spores from the forest next to it, which is poison to more delicate crops. It was not the wisest placement. Mostly the field is only good for growing hallen weed."*

"That's a sturdier plant?" Warin asked.

"It grows almost anywhere. But it's not good for much. Fabric-making, mostly. There is a juice that some make from the leaves, but it's very bitter. I think it's disgusting."

They reached the fence at the edge of the village, and Frellanda hopped the fence in one sharp move, sliding down the short embankment to the path below. They reached back up toward Warin. *"Do you need assistance?"* they asked.

"I can manage." Warin climbed over the fence more methodically and stepped down on the small strip of level ground the other side. He used his own momentum to half-run down the embankment, coming to a stop nearly in the large native's arms.

"A farmer's shortcut," Frellanda said to him. *"Much faster than going through the entrance and then around half the village."*

"You should think about putting in some stairs and a small gate," Warin said.

The native flicked their head. *"It's frowned upon, coming this way,"* they said. *"But that is not a bad idea."*

They walked along the outside of the village until they got to an intersection and turned onto a path between the fields. In the one to the right small purple sprouts had already started to punch through the ground in orderly rows.

"The juvvah roots," Frellanda said. *"They took to the ground very quickly this season. We planted them only days ago and they already reach to the suns. It bodes well for the harvest."*

They reached an intersection at the corner of four fields, and Frellanda stopped. They turned to the right and pointed down the path behind Warin. *"There is Ollahnah, minding the children as they plant."*

Warin turned around and looked. All he could see was a vague shape of a native against the fence in the distance. "Are you sure that's them?"

"I see them clearly," they replied. *"I hope the old one will be pleased to see you."*

"I hope so too," Warin said.

"I must go back to work in the next field," they said. *"There is so much of the ground that needs to be turned before the suns set. So I must leave you here."*

Warin nodded. "All right. Thank you for guiding me. And your hospitality. Letting me into your home."

"It was my privilege," they said. They rested their farming hoe on their torso as they held out their hands, palms facing him.

"Be well, friend Warin, and I hope you will honor my family with a visit again soon."

Warin held out his hands, copying their gesture. "I will," he said. "Thank you."

Frellanda took their farming hoe in their hands and turned, bounding off at speed into the next field. They hopped the fence with remarkable ease and joined with the other natives, who were swinging down hard into the ground.

Ollahnah rested against the fence, their eyes on the field where a dozen or more young natives were working. They turned to face Warin as he approached, and put their hands up. "Wahrin. Joolid," they verbalized.

Warin covered the headset microphone with his hand and replied, "Ollahnah. Joolid." Then he uncovered the microphone and continued through the translator, "I am glad to see you again."

Ollahnah reared back as the translator spoke. *"What is this strange voice you have now?"* they asked.

Warin explained the translator to them. The old native reached out and tapped it with a fingertip. *"Such a marvel,"* they said. *"Now you can make yourself understood much more easily."*

"I can," Warin said.

Ollahnah bobbed their head. *"I told the others you were not simple."*

"I appreciate that," Warin said with a laugh. "And I appreciate how you tried to help me before I got it. Teaching me words."

Ollahnah flailed their hands in front of them. *"The others didn't believe you couldn't understand them. They thought you were only pretending so you would be left alone. I didn't think that was true."*

"It wasn't." Warin patted the old retty on the arm. "So, thank you for trying."

The old retty grunted and looked away.

Warin noticed another of the large farming hoes like Frellanda's resting on the fence in front of them. "Is that yours?"

The old native grabbed it off the fence and held it out to Warin. *"Yes, this is my soilturn. I used it in these fields for many seasons."*

"Is that what you call it? A soilturn?"

"Yes, we use them for turning the ground, to ready it for seed." Ollahnah held out the large tool to Warin. *"Here."*

Warin reached out for the soilturn. His fingers barely enclosed its circumference. Ollahnah let go, and the full weight of it unexpectedly made him nearly drop it.

"Careful, friend Warin," Ollahnah said.

He wrapped his other hand around it and twisted it in the air to hold it in front of himself like a staff. The soilturn was a good half-meter taller than he was. Its surface was a dark reddish color, and very smooth—he could barely feel any of the wood's corkscrew grain. Here and there along its body were bumps where branches had been cut off the main body, making it look like it had been a small tree ripped out of the ground. Which it probably had been. The wood had been treated and aged and felt as solid as rock. At the top of it was a dark gray stone, a thick blade angled to one side, tied fast into a notch at the top of the wood. He turned it horizontally in his hands, straining unexpectedly to stop its momentum when it was horizontal. The stone blade made it very unbalanced.

Warin rested the soilturn back against the fence. "It's quite the impressive tool," he said. "You used it in the fields?"

"For many, many seasons," Ollahnah said, turning back to watch the field. *"In my youth, I could turn a whole field for*

planting by myself. I was the strongest farmer in the village." They stroked the soilturn gently. "*Those days are gone now. My strength is not what it once was. And my limbs are stiff. Now all I can do is watch the young as they work. I bring this with me to the field out of habit.*"

"You miss it."

Ollahnah flicked their head. "*I am honored and revered. I teach the young how to work the fields, how to best feed their families. It is my role now. I am not useless. There is a great pride in seeing how well they learn from me. And a great comfort in seeing how they will succeed after I am back in the ground.*" They were unmoving for a long moment, then: "*Still, I would prefer my strength.*"

Warin turned to watch the young in the field. They worked in even rows from back to front. Each had a pouch draped across their torso, which they would reach into for a handful of seed to sift into the ground in a line. When their hand was empty, they would reach down, cover the seeds with soil, and take a few steps forward and repeat the process. They all moved awkwardly, Warin thought, their actions somewhat exaggerated. Near the back one of the smaller children had stopped altogether, crouching down to play in the dirt with their fingers. Ollahnah grunted loudly, and it echoed across the field. The child looked up and then quickly got back to work.

None of them looked to be very large, at least by retty standards. Warin guessed at most they were half his height. He turned to Ollahnah. "How old are they?"

"*These children are all in their second season since birth. Their first planting.*"

"They're two years old?"

"*All the young take part in planting. It is how they learn the value of the farm. But we keep the youngest to the easy crops.*

Hallen weed is very simple. In truth, they do not even need to cover the seed. Scatter it however you want and it would still grow. But we use it to teach them how to plant the other crops the right way."

"I guess that makes sense," Warin said, shaking his head.

"It is only one day, friend Warin. Tomorrow they will be back at play with their—"

Suddenly, Ollahnah tensed. They raised off the fence and stared intently off into the field.

"What is it?" Warin asked.

Ollahnah pointed off to the far corner. Warin followed their hand. The field at the far end was bordered by the edge of a thick forest that continued all the way to the foot of the mountains in the distance. At the border he could just make out something dark gray coming out from the trees and sliding through the fence onto the field. It was easier to see against the backdrop of the field soil, but was still just an indistinct blur at this distance. But it was moving closer. Quickly.

"Is that an… animal?" he asked.

"It's a bool," Ollahnah said. *"Come down from the mountain."*

"Are they dangerous?"

The old retty didn't answer. They scampered over the fence and started towards the children in the field as quickly as their stiff body could manage. They turned to face him, their milky eyes wide. *"Stay here, friend Warin. I must gather the children."*

Ollahnah made their way out into the field, waving their arms and making a barking sound to get the children's attention. The children looked up at them but did not move. Ollahnah kept barking, getting closer. The bool kept advancing as well. It was close enough now that Warin could make out a basic shape of it. Still not with much detail, but it made him think of a wolf.

The beast let out a yelping sound that echoed throughout

the field. The children turned and started running toward Ollahnah, dropping their pouches as they did. The old native pushed at the first to reach them, to make them keep going onto the other field where the other farmers were working, as Ollahnah ran on to try and get between the children and the animal.

The beast sped up.

"RUN!" Warin yelled from the fence. It was clear to Warin that Ollahnah would not make it in front of all the children. They were fast and running with fright, but the beast was closing on them too rapidly. One child had started too late, having not realized what was going on. Another was limping along very slowly. The beast seemed to nod at each of them, trying to pick its target as it continued rapidly running, before deciding which of the children it wanted to go for. The slow one.

Before he even knew what he was doing, Warin was in the field running at full speed, carrying the soilturn in his hands like a lance. The ground was soft and unstable, and he nearly stumbled many times before he adjusted. His breath became shallow and weezy in his throat pretty quickly, and his legs started to burn, but he pushed past it and kept running. Up ahead of him he saw Ollahnah stumble and fall, desperately trying to get back up onto his feet, but slowly and in pain. He flew past them and kept going. The beast was nearly on top of the child.

The bool leaped at the fleeing child and grazed their shoulder, knocking them to the ground and landing past them. The child went to rise but the beast turned and jabbed at them with its snout, sending them back to the dirt. The child rolled away and tried again, managing to get to their feet for a few steps before the beast jumped on their back, pushing them down to the ground again. The child huddled into a ball, covering their face. The beast snarled, jabbing its head at the child, grabbing and ripping at their tunic.

The stone head of the soilturn caught the beast on the side of the head. Only a glancing blow, but enough to knock it off the child. The beast yelped and flew backward, running a short distance away and turning. Warin hopped over the child on the ground and stopped, holding out the soilturn in front of him, breathing hard.

"Run," he said to the child behind him. "Run to Ollahnah."

Warin didn't turn to see if the child obeyed. Vaguely he heard a scurrying behind him, but his focus was on the beast in front of him the other side of his staff.

The bool was large, with thick, dirty gray fur bunched up on its shoulders. It rested heavily on two large front legs bending outwards from its body, and a single muscular leg in the back. It stared at him with a solid black eye in the center of its sloping head. Thick lines of saliva dripped from its circular mouth, where sharp teeth from four sides ground against each other.

The beast danced in front of him, making a sound like a high-pitched growl. It didn't seem to know what to make of him. Warin jabbed the soilturn at it forcefully, hoping to scare it off. But the bool avoided it easily, swatted at it almost playfully. The tool was far too heavy for Warin to control well. And the beast did not look to be retreating. It moved closer to him a step at a time.

He was pretty sure he could not outrun it. And fighting it off… He thought of the pistol he had left behind in his tent derisively. One quick blast would have dealt with it. But with this cumbersome gardening tool, about the only thing he could think he'd be able to do was not make it easy on the damn thing.

With no warning, the bool suddenly charged. Warin swung the soilturn at it, hoping to knock it over, but the beast blocked it with its leg and stepped on it down to the ground, the force of its weight on the tool nearly pulling it out of Warin's hands. Before he could blink the beast jumped on him and knocked him over.

His head bounced off something hard, and the world was a blur in which he lost a few seconds. Still moving, still living, but not really aware. He almost went deeper into the fog, but his mind snapped back into the present when he felt hot spittle drip onto his cheek.

The bool was on top of him. Somehow he had managed to keep hold of the soilturn, and he held the beast off of him with it across its neck, pinning its legs up by its face. Razor-sharp claws extended from both paws. He pushed his legs into its torso, trying to kick it off of him. The jaw snapped just centimeters from his face. He turned his head to the side, away from it, closing his eyes, but could still hear the snapping of its teeth, feel its breath on his cheek. His arms started to give way under the weight of it. He felt a sharp pain in his temple as something cut him, one of its teeth or a claw, and he pushed it back from him with all his strength. It soon faded and the beast got closer again. Another stinging pain in his cheek. This time he didn't have the strength left to push back.

He started to feel distant from the whole experience, as if his mind was leaving his body before the inevitable. He still felt the pain, the soreness, but it was somehow not his anymore, not really. There was no panic or fear in him; those were things for someone else. Oddly, he thought, mostly what he felt was a little incredulous that this was how it was going to end for him.

Then abruptly something flew over him, and the weight was gone. There was no more pressure. His arms collapsed uselessly at his sides, and he felt nothing, no ripping at his face or body. Only the soilturn that fell across his chest.

He opened his eyes slowly and saw the empty field all the way to the distant fence, out of focus but there. He heard something squeal off to his right, followed by the sound of something hard cracking. With some effort he turned his head to follow the sound.

A few meters away the bool lay on its side, its legs flailing in the air as if desperately trying to grab purchase. One of its paws flapped randomly, the leg snapped in two. It was what was making the squealing sound. The beast's body lay crumpled underneath thick hooves. Warin glanced up and saw Frellanda standing on top of the beast, staring down at it. The bool looked a pathetic mess, no longer the monstrous beast millimeters away from ending his life.

Frellanda lifted up their leg from the shoulder of the beast, no longer in any condition to try to break free. The hoof came down hard directly on the bool's head, crushing its skull with a loud crack. The bool stopped moving and became inanimate.

Warin let out a long breath, feeling relieved, and passed out.

Ten

WARIN OPENED HIS EYES. Everything was dark; a fuzzy, reddish-orange haze. He blinked several times to try and focus. The orange glow moved around rhythmically. There were odd shapes in it, black stick figures. They looked like they were dancing. Or maybe they were just cracks in the surface. Or shadows. As his wits slowly came back to him, he registered what he was looking at—firelight reflecting off the inner wall of a native dome. He was laying on his back.

He moved to sit up and immediately regretted it, as the blood started to pound in his skull. He dropped back down with a groan. At least what he was lying on was soft. A cot of some kind, he thought. He heard it creak when he moved.

"Wahrin," said a voice next to him. He looked over and saw a retty sitting on the ground near his feet. Their features were in half-silhouette from the small fire in the center of the dome behind them.

"Rawilline," Warin said as he got up more slowly this time to face them.

The native bowed their head. "Hehllo." Rawilline held out the translator headset to him. "Tahk."

Warin vaguely remembered the device getting knocked off his head as the animal had jumped on him. He grabbed it and looked it over, holding it up to a candle burning on a table next to his cot.

There were scuff marks here and there. The metal headband looked like it had been warped, then hastily bent back into general shape, as did the microphone, and the cushion on the left speaker had a small tear. There was also a sharp edge on a section of the monocle where a sliver had been chipped off. But all of that seemed cosmetic, and otherwise the device looked fine. Hopefully it was still functional.

He put the translator on and moved the monocle and microphone into place. "Does this thing still work? Can you understand me?"

Rawilline nodded once. *"Your tool still functions,"* they said. *"Friend Dav made sure it was not broken."*

Warin sighed in mild relief. "Tough little thing," he muttered. He looked around the room. The only other person in the dome was another native huddled over the central fire and grinding something in a large bowl. "Where am I?"

"In the healer's home," Rawilline replied. *"They mended your cuts. You have been asleep for many hours."*

Warin touched his cheek, wincing at the burning-hot line he felt just above his jaw. Something like dried mud covered the gash.

The other native grunted, approaching Warin. *"Do not scrape that off,"* they said to him, pointing at his face. They leaned down and turned Warin's head to the side, examining him. *"Your kind heals quickly. But it still has some mending to do. You can wash it away tomorrow."*

"Are you sure your medicine works on me?"

"I can see that it does," the healer said. *"Friend Dav was most impressed with it."*

Warin nodded. "Where is Dav?"

"*He spent all day today watching over you,* "Rawilline replied. "*Conferring with the healer on how to treat you. But he said he had to report in and get back to Edirilla. I told him I would stay with you until you woke.*" They paused, then added, "*I did not think it would take so long, though.*"

"Well, I would've come to sooner if I knew you were waiting." He stretched out his neck. "How is the kid? Are they all right?"

"*The child is fine, friend Warin,*" Rawilline replied. "*They were frightened, but they are resting in their home tonight and they are well. Because of you.*"

Warin stared down at the floor. "I'm glad to hear it," he mumbled.

"*That was quite the thing, fighting off a bool by yourself.*"

He waved his hand in the air. "It was nothing."

"*The strongest of us find them a challenge. But you are...*"

"The size of a child?"

Rawilline straightened. "*A large child,*" they said.

Warin smiled and shook his head. "I really love that your people understand humor." Warin slung his feet out from the cot onto the ground. His body was stiff and he moved slowly. "I didn't actually do all that well though, did I? The thing would have had me for lunch if Frellanda hadn't shown up when they did." He looked down at his bare feet, then at the floor around them. "Where are my shoes?"

"*You should rest until sunrise,*" the healer said to him. "*You have no broken bones and your cuts are mending, but you need to regain your strength.*"

"I intend to," Warin said. "But in my own tent if that's all right."

"*You are welcome in my home,*" they said, putting their hand out. "*And I would like to examine you again in the morning to make sure you are truly on the mend. I would not want something to happen to my first human human being patient.*"

"I appreciate the offer, but I'll be fine."

Rawilline turned to the healer, raising their hand. "*I will walk with him and see that our friend is all right.*"

The healer made a clucking sound, shaking their head. "*If you insist, and friend Rawilline will make sure you get there. But I want you to come back tomorrow as soon as you rise. Or I will come and find you.*"

Warin nodded. "Yes, doctor."

Just outside the healer's home, a crowd of rettys were milling about a campfire. As Warin stepped outside, they rose and encircled him. They reached out and touched him gently on the face and shoulders. Many of the native's outlines flashed in his monocle. "*You saved my child,*" came from his headset with one voice, though he suspected they were all saying it more or less together.

"It was nothing," he said, politely pushing their hands away. "Really."

A smaller retty cupped the top of his head in their hand and stared at him intently. "*My child would not be home right now resting without you. It is something.*" They reached into a satchel around their waist and pulled out a large stone figurine. They held it out to Warin. "*Please,*" they said, bowing slightly. "*A token of my gratitude.*"

Warin took the figurine, which was almost the length of his forearm. He looked at it in his hands. It was of a retty, staff in their left hand, their head up and staring into the distance, carved from a black, shiny rock like obsidian. The nearby fire glowed along its side, though he could only see a little of its detail in the dark. But he could feel the carefully crafted lines and contours in his fingers.

Rawilline stepped forward between him and the crowd. *"Friend Warin needs to rest,"* they said. *"Let him be for now."* They led Warin through the small crowd who parted for them.

As he passed by the one who had given him the figurine, Warin turned to them and said, "Thank you," quietly as he passed.

Retii 4 did not have a moon, but the system was situated more inside the Orion Arm in a dense cluster of stars, so was still well illuminated at night by a starscape at least triple what Earth had. There were no clouds in the night sky, so even as they moved toward the grove and away from the more populated area of the village, Warin did not feel blind, as he walked stiffly next to Rawilline, glancing down regularly at the figurine in his hands.

"That is Enaa the Traveler," Rawilline said. They bobbed their head. *"One of the six who founded our village. They wandered the world from the moment they could walk, and did not stay in any one place for more than a day. Their hooves touched every grain of sand, every petal of mossy forest floor, and mote of dirt in the world."*

"That is quite a lot of traveling," Warin said with a chuckle.

"No place was a happy home for them. Only when they came upon this valley did they find contentment, and their travels ended."

"Was Tyun already here?"

"None were here when Enaa came. They found this valley. Tyun came flying down from the mountains when Enaa called." Rawilline replied. *"You have been learning about our people."*

"Not much. Just that, really. Tyun's name."

"It is a wonderful story. You must hear the rest." Rawilline ran a finger along the side of Warin's figurine. *"It is an appropriate figure for you, as you are also a great traveler."* Rawilline stopped

walking and looked up at the night sky. *"Tell me, friend Warin, do you know which of these distant suns is your home?"*

Warin stopped and turned to Rawilline. "Dav told you?"

"Friend Dav only answered vaguely. I suspect he did not want to take time to explain further as it would mean less time for his own questions. Or that he worried we would not understand."

"Then how did you know?"

"In my youth I traveled too. Like Enaa. I stepped foot on the far-flung lands of my world, and spent many seasons away from home. And nowhere have I seen anything the likes of a human human being. And there are no tales of anything like your kind in any land of this world. Where else could you have come from, but one of these distant suns? Or perhaps closer?" Rawilline pointed at a red, twinkling point of light. *"There, are you from that neighbor? The one with the rings?"*

Warin looked at the native, surprised. He was pretty sure they were pointing at Retii 6, one of the gas giants in the system. From what he recalled it was massive, twice the size of Jupiter, with thick rings of rock and ice. Yet it was little more than a twinkling dot to his eyes. "You can actually see its rings?" Warin asked.

"They are faint and clearer in the winter, but yes. That one also circles our suns, does it not? That has always been what we thought."

"It does, yes. Hell, you're skipping right past Copernicus." Warin shook his head. "We really don't appreciate how good your vision is. Incredible." He sighed deeply. "But no, that is not our home. Our home is…" He turned in a slow circle scanning the sky, but then stopped. "Actually, I don't know. It's up there somewhere." He pointed to the northern sky. "Over there, perhaps? One of those faint lights on the edge of the spiral arm, very dim? Might not be able to see it even with your eyes. It could be over there. But I honestly don't know."

Rawilline grunted. *"You are farther from your home than I thought,"* they said.

"We are. It's a very long way away."

They walked again for a time in their own thoughts. When they reached the edge of the grove, Warin asked, "Does it bother you, knowing we come from another world?"

"I had always wondered if there were other lands around those distant suns. And others in those lands. I thought there might be. With so many suns above... But it seemed fanciful to think. Are there many others?"

"There are a few, yes."

Rawilline shook their head. *"Wondrous."* They sat down in the short grass, folding their hands in their lap. They looked upward again at the stars. *"I would like to meet them."*

Warin stood next to them, watching them as they stared upwards. "You amaze me, Rawilline. With how easily you accept this."

"You make it easy, friend Warin," they said. *"Risking your life as you did today showed that you are a true friend."*

Warin waved at them dismissively. "That was... You would have done the same thing."

Rawilline looked directly at Warin. *"Yes, I would have. For one of my own."*

Warin stared at Rawilline for a long moment before turning away.

Rawilline changed the subject. *"Tell, me, friend Warin: have you traveled much on my world?"*

Warin shook his head. "I've only been in this valley. Dav has, though. He's been all over both Llama and Lamb."

Rawilline twitched their head. *"What are those?"*

"Oh, right, that's the name we gave your other continents. Llama the large one in the east, Lamb the one in the west. And this one we call Lorca. It's not their official names, just sort of what we call them. Nicknames, I guess. What are they actually called?"

"The great one in the east, where we all came from, that is Gregan. The west, where we moved next, that is Verut. And our land here is Oohilt. You truly have never been to any of them?"

"Only this valley," Warin replied.

"You have missed many a great sight, friend Warin."

Warin shrugged. "I'm just a scribe. Dav is the one who travels."

"I know. I have talked with friend Dav at length about the northern lands. He is a great studier of us from afar." Rawilline silently stared at Warin for a long time, then, *"He knows of the great sickness that has ravaged Gregan and Verut. And has reached our lands as well. Do you know of it?"*

Warin's heart jumped. "Yes."

"We have only heard what traveling merchants have told us. How death rolls through the villages and towns, leaving none in their wake. No one has heard from our kin in Gregan or Verut in over a season, and their boats do not come over the oceans anymore. And none sail there, or if they do, they do not return. Most here do not believe it, think it is just a tale. It is soon forgotten. Especially now, as we have had no traveling merchants visit us in many days to talk of it. In fact, no one has come through the pass at all this spring. Or for some time before it."

Warin took a deep breath. "What did Dav tell you?"

"He doesn't speak of it. But I can see in his face the subject clearly pains him. Just like I see it does for you."

Warin turned away from Rawilline. Even in the dark the native could read him.

Rawilline grunted at Warin, making him turn to face them. The native continued. *"Please, friend Warin. Tell me, is the sickness near?"*

Warin closed his eyes. There was no point in trying to lie. He nodded to the retty. "Yes. It's reached the towns on the other side of the valley. And all the land around us."

"And what of all the people?"

"They're gone."

Rawilline was motionless for a long time, staring at Warin. He felt like shrinking under their gaze. Finally the native bobbed their head and looked away. *"And now it comes for us,"* they said.

Rawilline stared off at the dark silhouette of the mountains behind Warin. In the distance, something howled.

Warin stepped closer to Rawilline and placed a hand on their arm. "I'm sorry," Warin said.

Rawilline patted his hand gently. *"I know you are, friend Warin."* They stood up and faced back into the village. *"The death of the old or the sick, that is hard enough to accept. My own demise too is hard to believe, no matter how true its inevitability is. But I will be planted and my bones will feed, and more will be born and live, and grow. Someone will take my place, and the world continues. I can see it, I can understand it. But the nd of all of my people, all that we are and all we have done. All gone. The weeds will grow over our land and homes, and the harvest will rot in the ground. Everything will fade. Even if we are put in the field, there will be no children to feed. The end of us is the true end. It is a very hard thing to grasp."* Rawilline looked at Warin. He thought their face looked weary. *"How long do we have?"*

"I don't know."

"Can you do anything to help us?"

"Yes."

Warin said it so abruptly he made himself jump. Rawilline even seemed taken aback, blinking hard at him several times. He hadn't thought about the question, what Rawilline had asked him. Or what his answer meant, what he was committing to. He had just answered. Had he meant it? It seemed he did. He wanted to. And the more he thought about it, the more certain he became.

"Yes," he repeated. "Yes I will."

Eleven

WARIN HUSTLED THROUGH the streets of the midday village so intently that he nearly missed Ollahnah greeting him as he passed by the well. The old native outstretched their hands to Warin. Warin did the same and stopped.

"Ollahnah. Joolid," he said, cupping his headset's microphone.

"Wahrin. Joolid," they replied verbally, then continued normally. *"Welcome to such a fine day."*

"Thank you," Warin replied. "I'm afraid I can't stay and talk. I have to meet Dav at the village gate."

Ollahnah nodded. *"This is the day your friends are coming, yes?"*

"It is. And I'm late already."

"Then I won't keep you. Here." Ollahnah pulled a small sack from their satchel. *"This is a gift for them. And you."*

Warin took the sack and opened it. Inside were several small spear-shaped red vegetables. He looked up at the old native. "Unna roots?"

"My grandchild pulled them this morning," Ollahnah said. *"I hope your friends like them."*

"I'm sure they will. Thank you." Warin closed the sack. "But you didn't have to get them anything."

"Ah, but they should be made as welcome here as you are, friend

Warin. What little I could do to help, I will. You must bring them back here. I am eager to meet them. As many of us are. Undallin had said they would have a gift for your friends as well. But they are not here. Nor are their siblings." Ollahnah looked around. *"I'm not sure where they are."*

"I'm sure they're just running late. Like I am." Warin started to walk away, then turned back to the old native. "I'll bring them by to meet you. Promise. They'll want to thank you for the gift."

Warin took one of the unna roots out of the bag and nibbled on it as he continued on. It had a pleasant, almost tangy taste, that Warin likened to a sweet potato. Though the texture was much crisper than that, more like a granny smith apple he had once from a station arboretum as a kid. The root grew wild outside the village like a weed of sorts among bushes and trees. To hear Ollahnah talk of them they were an acquired taste—a favorite of the old native's, but many rettys did not care for them at all. He suspected they weren't particularly nutritious either. More of a treat than a meal. But he had been so wrapped up in searching the Ministry database since he woke up that he had forgotten to eat breakfast, so they were still welcome.

The streets were not as crowded as usual, so it didn't take as long to get to the front gate as he had thought it would. He half-jogged the last few dozen meters, scanning past the archway. The road was empty all the way to the distant turn around the hills, with no sign of the jeep. A very small group of rettys stood milling about the entrance, interacting with each other in small circles, occasionally glancing down the road. Nowhere near the number of natives that had been at the gate when Dav and Warin had arrived, which he thought was a little odd. Less interest the second time, Warin guessed. Though just as before, Edirilla and Rawilline stood in front of them all, stoically waiting. Except now Dav stood next to them, his hands clasped behind his back.

Warin stopped to stand next to Dav, who turned and nodded at him, then went back to watching the road. Edirilla and Rawilline, standing on the other side of the xenologist, turned and offered a more formal greeting, and Warin returned the gesture.

"Any word from them?" he asked Dav, muting the headset.

"They just got on the road near where we met Tyundelorro," Dav replied. "Still insisting on driving the whole way here."

"It's not that big of a deal, is it?"

"Maybe not," Dav said with a sigh. "I still wish they would have left the jeep out of sight and walked in. I doubt I have a good enough grasp of the retty's verbal language to have adequately described the concept of a motorized vehicle to them. Best I could come up with is 'cart with no harness.' They probably think that means they push it."

"Do you want me to say something to them now?" Warin asked, tapping the headset.

Dav shook his head. "I doubt it would make much of a difference. It's probably a little beyond them to grasp it anyway."

Warin almost replied to that but changed the subject instead. "How are the language lessons coming?"

"Fine," he replied. "Immersion is always the best way. It is a little cumbersome, though."

"Yeah, I got that impression. Having different words for the same thing depending on how you are using it can get tough."

Dav shook his head. "That's not a problem. There are plenty of old human languages that did the same thing. It's more that their verbal language is not very intricate. It isn't the primary language, after all. But beyond that, from a purely physiological perspective, the rettys don't have our vocal range."

"Vocal range?"

"Yes. Human beings have forty-four different sounds we can make for verbal communication. The rettys have barely more than half that. And they also don't have the dexterity in their mouths or their vocal cords to vary pitch or tone all that much. So they don't have the same range to communicate aurally that we do. Which means saying something, sometimes even something basic, can mean a lot of combining multiple sounds in a long string. Which can make everything get cumbersome."

"So it's not very efficient?"

"It's not. It can almost be like needing to spell out every word in a sentence to say it."

"Sounds fun."

Dav shrugged. "The lack of intricacy does make it easier to pick up, at least. There's a lot less of a base to memorize first."

Edirilla turned to Dav. *"Your friends approach,"* they said verbally to the xenologist, which Warin's headset translated.

Warin looked down the road. He couldn't make anything out at first, or perhaps just a vague dark smudge. Then he saw a flash of something metal rise from the ground at the peak in the road, followed by a tan-colored blur that stood out against the grass of the hills and fields behind it. Definitely the jeep. It continued onward, getting slowly larger as it approached. When it had traversed half the ground from the hill, he could start to hear the whir of its engine faintly.

Rawilline turned to Warin. *"This is the vehicle your friends use?"* they asked him.

Warin unmuted his headset as he nodded. "That's them. Don't be alarmed at it."

"There is no alarm." They glanced at Dav briefly, then back to him. *"It's just we thought friend Dav was making it up when he explained it."*

Warin smiled and didn't reply.

The jeep pulled off to their right and stopped. A few of the rettys nearby approached the jeep, though none came close enough to touch it. The front passenger-side door opened, making a few of them jump back. Rek stepped out tentatively.

Warin walked up to Rek, who was staring at the rettys, his mouth open. "Glad you could make it," he said to him.

Rek glanced at him quickly and then back at the rettys. "Yeah, sorry it took a bit longer than we thought. The jeep had some trouble finding a safe incline into the fields."

Lil stepped out of the back and Bela exited from the other side of the vehicle. Neither acknowledged Warin as they too stared at the natives.

"Gare didn't come?" Warin asked.

"She stayed back up at the base," Rek replied. "She didn't want to leave the observation post unmanned."

"Really? The base can't go a day or two on autopilot?"

"Not supposed to."

"Ministry rules," Bela added.

"I guess." Warin cleared his throat. "So," he said to the three of them. "What do you think of my new friends?"

Lil gripped the top of her open jeep door, almost as if she was holding it up in front of her. "They're so... big."

"And friendly," Warin said. "Come on, I'll introduce you. I think channel four on the comms tunes to my translator so you can understand them."

"We won't need that," Bela said, turning her head to the side. In her right ear she had an earphone with a small microphone head ending in the middle of her cheek. Both Rek and Lil had them as well.

"New version," Rek said. Warin saw a slight discoloration in his right eye from a contact lens.

"Dav told us about the translator," Lil said. "It was easy to find in the printer's memory. Of course, I had to improve on the design first."

"Naturally," Warin said.

Edirilla welcomed them into the village with the same brief-yet-still-formal words they had used for Dav and Warin. Rek took the nominal lead in replying, as Lil was distracted by gawking at everything around them, and Bela seemed bored. Warin thought her whole demeanor seemed strange; distant, disinterested, almost actively so. She barely seemed to notice the rettys that had crowded around them as Edirilla spoke. Not at all the same kind of barely contained excitement that was all over Lil and Rek's faces. *That* you would expect in a biologist getting to meet her subjects for the first time. Warin tried to get her eye but she wouldn't look his way. After Edirilla had finished their welcome to the new visitors, she walked off with Dav and Edirilla before he could speak to her.

Much of the crowd of natives went with them, including Rawilline. A few natives stayed behind, mostly milling about the jeep. Rek politely worked around them as he locked the vehicle down.

Warin approached Lil at the back of the jeep. She grabbed a heavy pack in both her hands from the trunk and slung it onto her shoulders. "Where have you been staying?" she asked him.

"I set up my tent at the far end of the village. In a grove of trees."

"Not in one of their homes?"

Warin shrugged "I prefer the privacy. Dav is staying with the chief, so you can do something like that too if you want." He held out the sack of roots to Lil. "Treat?"

Lil looked in the bag. "What is it?"

"They call it unna root. They're not bad."

Lil grabbed one and took a small bite. She chewed it for a minute very carefully, before nodding and taking a larger bite.

Warin stepped closer to her. "Listen," he said quietly. "About the other day—"

Lil shook her head. "Forget it."

"No really, I'm sorry I implied you hacked me. I was jumping to conclusions I shouldn't have. It definitely must have been a glitch of some kind."

Lil shrugged. "It'd be an oddly specific computer glitch to get, but whatever."

"Well that's what I called it in the report I filed. Just some kind of weird computer glitch." Warin glanced over at Rek. He was around the front of the jeep, dealing with the windshield cover. He reached into his pocket and pulled out a small memory stick. "Kind of like the one that made this."

Lil took the stick and turned it over in her hand. "What's on here?"

"A copy of Dav's notes on the villagers. Everything he's learned since we've been on this trip."

She looked up at Warin. "You hacked Dav's account?"

Warin shook his head. "Didn't need to. All three of them often put their field notes into a working subdirectory. It's protocol. I have access to it too."

"And you're giving it to me why?"

"I thought it would be pretty useful for someone who was planning on leaking data about the rettys to the public," Warin said. "If you knew of someone looking to spark a public outcry against the Ministry."

Lil put the stick in her pocket. "Seems a crazy risk to take for something I could just grab myself. I mean, all this data is going to be in his reports."

Warin smiled. "Well first, you didn't even know the

subdirectory existed, so you wouldn't know to look for it. And second, this is more than just a report: this is all the data he's gotten on them. Their language, culture, technology. Everything, all in one place, not spread out over who knows how many reports he'll end up filing. And you have all of it now."

Lil stared at the ground, slowly nodding. When she looked back up at him she said, "Decided to get off the sideline, huh?"

"You could say that."

Lil picked up her pack and slung it over her shoulders. "All right. Thanks for this. I can make sure this doesn't get back to you, but you should be careful on your end anyway. I take it you'll have more of this?"

"Probably. If I have time. There's something else I want to try too."

"What?"

"I want to talk to Bela first before I say anything."

Lil shook her head. "She's not interested. I already tried to talk to her. She blew me off."

"Well let me try. I got something a little more than leaking documents in mind."

Lil opened her mouth to say something, but Rek walked over just at that moment. "All locked up. You two ready? I'm dying to see this village."

THE THREE OF them caught up with the rest of the procession as it made its way to the tent, where Edirilla held court for the new visitors, much as they had when Dav and Warin had arrived. Again, each of them was given a plate of food. The meal was nothing new for Dav and Warin. Rek dived into his with very little hesitation, as did Bela. Lil eyed hers, uncertain. She had grown up and spent most of her life on stations just as Warin had, so like him she was not as used to natural food, alien or otherwise, as the others were. But as she saw how the rest of them were enjoying theirs she joined in, and her expression changed to pleasant surprise after a few bites.

The conversation over their meal was cordial, friendly. Edirilla and Rawilline did most of the speaking, answering what Rek or Lil asked about, but more asking questions of the newcomers, on things both in general and personal. Warin thought that both of the natives showed, while still very general, a surprisingly good grasp of humanity. They had gotten more information from Dav and himself than he had thought. And now they were taking full advantage of the presence of others who were not as evasive as Dav, as Rek, Lil, and to a lesser extent Bela, were happy to fill in any gaps they were asked about, and did not press so much with questions of their own. Dav watched the conversation quietly but didn't take part. Lil had offered the xenologist one of her improved translators, but he had stuffed it into his pocket, declining to use it.

After the meal had concluded, a younger retty approached Edirilla and spoke to them, placing their hands on both sides of their face, which was the native version of whispering. When the messenger had finished the chief stood from their stool quickly. *"It has been a great honor to have met all of you, but I have other duties to attend to today. Friend Warin, can you guide your friends?"*

"Of course," he said. "My pleasure."

The chief extended their hands out to them. *"May you be welcome in my home,"* they said, and turned from the bench and walked out the back of the tent, Rawilline and Dav following.

Warin turned to Bela, only to see her walking off to follow the natives and Dav without a word. "Where are you going?" Warin asked after her.

She glanced back at Warin with a smirk, shaking her head, but said nothing and left.

"She's been like that for a few days now," Rek said. "Even more distant than normal. Don't take it personally."

"Fine," Warin said with a little shrug. He turned back to Lil and Rek. "So what do you two want to see first?"

"You're the one who knows the place," Rek said.

"Okay. Then let's start at one of the wells. They're a sort of meeting place for the natives. There's someone I want you to meet there."

"Is there someplace to drop off our packs first?" Lil asked as she lifted hers from the ground in front of her.

Warin led them to his tent in the grove, where they dropped off their packs. "It's a nice spot and a little secluded," he said as they arrived. "The rettys don't come into this section much. You can set up your tents here."

Lil shook her head. "I'm not sure if I'm staying overnight."

"No?"

"I have things to do back up at the base, and I could relieve Gare. She should get a chance to visit too," she replied. "And besides, I'm not a great fan of camping."

"You could always stay with one of the natives," Rek said to her. "It probably won't be as comfortable as your own bed, but I'm sure one of them would have a nice cot for you in the corner."

Lil glared at him but didn't reply, leaning her pack against a tree.

Rek dropped his own pack, and noticed the figurine sitting just outside Warin's tent. "That's an interesting piece," he said. "Can I see it?"

Warin picked it up and handed it to him. "It's one of the village founders. One of the rettys gave it to me as a gift."

Rek turned the figurine over in his hands. "Very nice," he said. "Hold on a sec. Let me get an image of it."

Rek fished around in his pack with his free hand. He pulled out a holocam and circled the object with it, letting its laser points run up and down the figurine's surface as he held it gingerly in his hand. The holocam beeped when it had acquired enough surface detail, and he put it back in his pack. Rek handed the figurine back to Warin.

"For the records," he said.

They made their way very slowly through the village. Both Lil and Rek meandered and could not stop looking around at all the rettys who watched them as they passed. But their pace was mostly because of Rek, who stopped continuously, picking up stones and pebbles from the ground to look over, occasionally taking a sample reading with his spectrometer before tossing it back to the ground. The rettys watched him as he worked. Once or twice a native would pick up a rock he had just discarded and look it over carefully.

"Finding anything interesting?" Warin asked him.

Rek shook his head. "Nothing I didn't already know. Igneous rocks, mostly—traces of copper, nickel, palladium, osmium. And platinum—a little more of that this far down from the mountains than I would have thought."

"Platinum?" Lil asked.

Rek turned to her. "Oh yeah, most of the mountains around here are full of it. In an Industrial Age civilization, this whole valley would be a huge mining hub."

"How lovely," Lil said snidely and turned away.

As the three of them wandered, Warin kept glancing around, slightly distracted. He vaguely realized he was doing it, just as he also knew he was doing it in the hope of spotting Edirilla, Rawilline, and Dav, but more particularly Bela. It wasn't that he expected to see any of them around the next turn in the path or around the corner of the next hut. The village wasn't so small to expect that. But twice since they had arrived Bela had blown him off, avoided talking to him. And more than anyone else he wanted to talk to her. Her avoiding him only seemed to intensify that.

Ollahnah was still at the neighborhood well when Warin returned with Rek and Lil. The old native held out their hands to them as they approached. *"You are back, friend Warin,"* they said.

"I told you I would be," he replied. He turned to the side and gestured to his two companions who looked at the old native, smiling. "These are my friends, Lil and Rek. This is Ollahnah."

"Nice to meet you," Lil said, stepping forward with her hand outstretched.

Ollahnah looked down at her hand. *"Ah, the human human being greeting."* They took her hand and shook it gently. *"Well met, friend Lil. You are a woman?"*

Lil blinked deeply. "Well, yes. I am."

Ollahnah shook their head. *"Warin told me about your kind. Such a strange idea. He and she."*

"You don't know the half of it," Lil said, raising an eyebrow.

Ollahnah let go of her hand and turned to Rek. *"Well met, friend Rek."*

Rek shook the old native's hand. "Likewise. Warin told us you were the one who gave him the unna roots."

"Did you like them?"

Rek nodded quickly with a sharp upturn of his chin. "Yes. Thank you for them." Rek hadn't, actually. Back at the gate he had taken a small bite of one and blanched. He finished it, slowly, but left the rest of the bag for Lil and Warin. Warin realized he had not mentioned to either of them how a retty, such as Ollahnah, who had spent a good deal of time with a human like himself would be very adept at reading human expressions.

Even with their failing eyesight. But if the old native noticed something different in Rek's face as opposed to what he said, they didn't mention it.

Warin turned to Ollahnah. "Would it be all right if I left these two with you?"

Ollahnah turned to him and nodded. *"Of course. I am honored by their company."*

Rek turned to Warin. "Where are you going?" he asked.

"I just remembered, I need to talk to Dav and Bela about something," he replied.

"What?"

"Just a few odds and ends about their reports recently." He took a few steps away. "I'll catch up with you later."

Rek shrugged his acquiescence and turned back to Ollahnah, who had pulled out more unna roots from his satchel. Lil was chewing on one with a smile.

WARIN FOUND BELA by herself in the healer's home, standing in front of a long table holding three rows of the healer's collected herbs and medicines. As he stepped through the opening, she was holding up a purplish leaf to the light coming through the skylight and turning it over in her hand. He knocked on the hard side of the entrance.

Bela looked over at him. "How'd you find me?"

"I asked around. You stand out."

Bela shrugged and turned away again, putting the leaf into a small glass jar, sealing it, and dropping it onto a bag on a table in front of the healer's medicine rack.

"Where are the others?" Warin asked.

"The healer had to go on a house call," she replied, not turning around. "Dav and the others went with them."

"You didn't go too?"

"I'm not a traveling doctor." She grabbed a stone container from the medicine rack and looked inside. "I'm a researcher."

"So you're…"

"Collecting samples. The healer said I could take as many as I wanted. So I am."

He walked over to stand next to her at the table. "I hope you're not cleaning them out."

Bela took an empty glass jar from her bag and sprinkled the contents of the stone container into it. "I don't need that much. Not that it matters. Most of this stuff is probably nothing, a placebo at best."

"Then why take them?"

She sealed the glass jar and dropped it into her bag. "Because it's my job." Bela turned and faced him. "What do you want, Warin?"

"I was just checking in. We didn't get a chance to talk when you arrived."

"And what do we have to talk about?"

"The other night."

"What about it?"

Warin stepped closer. "The way we left it. I shouldn't have been so dismissive of what you were saying. About the rettys. And I didn't mean to come off like I was telling you your job. I'm sorry."

Bela shook her head. "You think that bothered me?"

"Didn't it? You kind of just got up and left your own bedroom."

Bela almost laughed. "Because I wanted to take a shower before going down to the lab." She turned back to the table. "I wasn't mad at you, Warin. I'm not mad at you now. You are who you are, and it's fine. So you can be a little annoying and patronizing. I've known men with worse flaws. You're still a fun distraction and great for stress relief. Which is nice. But I don't have time for you right now."

"Oh really?" Warin said. "What are you so busy with? You haven't filed any reports recently. Or done anything Ministry-related in over a week. I'd know."

Bela stopped in mid-grab of another container but didn't say anything.

Warin continued. "Look. Say what you want, but I know I pissed you off. And I'm sorry. I was wrong to be so dismissive. And I was wrong about everything I said. About the rettys, about the Ministry. Being down here, it's opened my eyes. These rettys, they're people, life forms, and they're more important than some stupid Ministry guideline. There are things we can do to save them." Warin glanced at the doorway, then around the room, before turning back to Bela. "And maybe we should do them."

Bela turned back to Warin slowly. "Should we, now?"

Warin nodded. "Didn't you tell me there were three things in the lab right now that could 'stop the Bug cold'? I think that's the way you put it."

Bela crossed her arms. "And if there is?"

"What are they?"

"What good would knowing do you?"

"I'm not completely stupid, Bela. I have to have a basic knowledge of all your fields to do my job."

"Does this basic knowledge of yours cover mass inoculation dispersal methods? You think you just get a bunch of needles and prick all the rettys you see?"

"Well, what about aerosol delivery?" Warin asked. "Fly a drone over the village with it."

Bela snorted. "That is way beyond your abilities."

"Could you do it?" Warin asked.

"Easily."

"So do it."

Bela shook her head and turned away from Warin again. Warin put a hand on her shoulder and turned her back to him. "Okay, fine, you don't want to get into trouble. You don't want to risk your career. So just tell me how to do it. Just the basics. Point me to the right files in the database. You don't have to be involved beyond that. If I get caught—"

Bela shook his arm off her. "You would get caught almost immediately."

"I don't care. They can do what they like to me. But they'll never know you helped. I'll tell them I worked it all out on my own."

"And you think anybody would believe a bureaucrat with no real scientific training managed to create a complex vaccine and secretly disperse it all on their own?"

"I find the right files on the database, why couldn't I? I can follow instructions. And the microbial printer in your lab is not that complicated. The Ministry finds out they'll just think I got lucky."

"Yeah, Warin, because manufacturing vaccines, it's that simple. It's like a recipe for a carrot cake."

Warin stepped closer. "Look, just point me in the right direction. Give me one thing to try. What do you care if I fail? You hate the nonintervention policy, don't you?"

"Of course I do. All that arbiters of life and death nonsense Gare keeps repeating. Anyone with a functioning brain could see it for the moral cowardice that it is."

"Then help me beat it."

Bela shook her head and looked at Warin with almost pity. "No, Warin."

Warin stared down at the table intently for a moment, leaning his fist on its surface. "I'm going to try with or without your help."

Bela turned away from Warin and leaned down on the table. "You can't do it without my help," she said. "And with my help it doesn't matter if you do it or not."

"Why not?"

"Because it's too late, Warin. Has been for some time."

"You don't know that. There could still be time."

"You sure?" Bela pulled out another container and sniffed it, wincing slightly, before putting it back.

"It hasn't spread into the valley yet, has it?" Warin said. "Maybe it won't. It can't get past the mountains. We're too isolated."

"Or maybe the mountains took a little longer to thaw this year than the models predicted, thus delaying the migration of the animals carrying the Bug into the valley by a few weeks."

Warin took a step back from her. "You don't know that's what happened."

Bela snorted. "Again with you telling me what I don't know. That's funny. All this biology, immunology, epidemiology, charting infection patterns. It's just what I do, Warin." Bela straightened up and turned to face him. "But all right, you want something less scientific. More anecdotal. How's this? What kind of a house call does a healer rush off to where the chief of the village and their second goes with them? Dav too? In such a hurry that they don't even notice or care that I didn't go with them?"

Warin stared at Bela hard but didn't say anything.

Bela smiled back at him, almost wickedly. "Looks like the valley wasn't as much of a barrier as you've convinced yourself into thinking it was."

Twelve

REK AND LIL were not still at the well when Warin returned. Ollahnah was nowhere to be seen either. Warin stopped at the side of the well and looked around. There were only a handful of rettys around, much less than he had been used to seeing in the locale during the day. The comparative emptiness of the space felt coldly unnerving to him.

He approached a pair of rettys nearby, a younger native standing over an elder who sat on a stump stool heavily. "Excuse me," he said, clearing his throat. "Could you tell me where my friends have gone? The two that are like me?"

The old native looked up at him. *"Are they not here?"* they said. The old native's head drooped back down. *"I did not see them leave."*

"Ollahnah took them to the village center," the younger retty said to Warin. *"To the first well."* They turned back to the older native next to them. *"You saw them leave, said goodbye to them."*

The old native shook their head. *"I do not remember."*

The younger retty placed a hand on their shoulder. *"I will take you home now. You need to rest."* They helped the old retty to their feet, turning back to Warin. *"My parent has been acting strange all day,"* they said to him. *"I do not know why."*

"I'm sure it's nothing," Warin said tightly.

Warin walked at a brisk pace through the heart of the village looking all around him. There were fewer rettys about, walking along or working outside their homes. More of the domes were dark and silent than he had seen before as well. Yet he did not sense any feeling of panic in any of the natives he saw, nothing felt out of the ordinary. Just that there were fewer of them around. He realized it had been like that all day, everywhere he had been since he left the grove that morning. But he had been so preoccupied with his own things he hadn't noticed.

He closed his eyes tight and took a deep breath to calm himself down. It didn't mean anything, he told himself. Not on its own.

When Warin arrived at the first well, he saw Rek leaning deep down into it, one foot off the ground. Ollahnah stood next to him holding on to his waist. Lil stood on the other side of the well watching the two of them, smirking.

Warin walked up to the well and peered in. In the dark shade of the inside of the well he could barely make out Rek leaning down against the side. A whirring sound echoed up to him. "What are you doing?"

Rek looked up at Warin. "Getting a sample."

"A sample of what?"

"The well." He replied. He turned back to the side of the well and pushed off with his hands. "Pull me back up," he shouted. Ollahnah gripped him by the back of his shirt and pulled him out of the well, leaving him standing upright next to Warin, his face a little red from being upside down. He held up a small device in his hand to Warin's face. "See?" he said. The device looked like some kind of tiny hand drill, with a tip on the end barely thicker than a hypodermic needle.

"What is it?" Warin asked.

"It's a core sample of the rock in the well's side." Rek smiled wide and removed the tip, putting the device in his pocket. "With this I can compare the outer layer of the stone, the weathering, oxidization, and whatnot on it to the inner matter, and with that difference date the well's construction. And as our friend here told me the village sprang up from this well, it'll tell us how old the village is."

"Shame you didn't fall in," Lil said.

Ollahnah placed a hand on Rek's shoulder. *"Would you truly wish calamity to befall friend Rek?"*

Lil raised her eyebrows and turned away, but did not say anything, looking at the homes at the edge of the village center.

Rek continued. "I had to get a sample from down inside the well. These outer rocks, they've clearly been replaced at some point. Totally different kind of stone. And the etchings in the sides are probably even newer than that. But the inner lining of the well below the ground level, that's likely original."

Warin nodded, only half-listening as he looked around the center. More rettys were milling about here, curious about the humans and watching them from a polite distance. None of them seemed to be in distress.

Warin turned to Ollahnah, who was watching with fascination as Rek placed the sample in a metal sleeve in his bag at the foot of the well. "Ollahnah, do you feel all right?" he asked the old native.

Ollahnah looked at him, cocking their head to the side. *"I am fine, friend Warin."*

"Are you sure? You don't feel tired, or run-down? Short of breath?"

"Not at all. Holding friend Rek was not a burden to me. You human human beings are as light as children."

Lil stepped around from the well. "Is something going on?"

Warin looked at her, and at Rek, who had straightened up and turned to him. Ollahnah looked at him as well, waiting for him to speak.

Warin let out a deep breath and shook his head with a smile.

"It's nothing. Everything's fine. Just Bela trying to get to me, I think." Warin shook himself and looked at Rek. "Anyway, what are you doing? I left you with Ollahnah to show you around, not for you to engage them in manual labor."

Rek raised his hands. "Ollahnah volunteered."

"They did," Lil said, putting her hand on the old native's arm. "Ollahnah has been very good to us. They have made us feel welcome."

"As you are, friend Lil."

"Well as long as they have not been taking advantage of you."

Ollahnah shook their head. *"Friend Rek and friend Lil are most enjoyable companions. I have never had such an interesting day."*

"I'm glad to hear it," Warin said. "Where have you shown them so far?"

"We visited the market by the grove, the jewelry stands, and the clothier."

"And the blacksmith," Rek said grinning. "Don't forget that one. That was my favorite."

"Oh please," Lil said, shaking her head.

Warin looked back and forth at the two of them. "What happened at the blacksmith's?"

Rek nodded at Lil. "She got us thrown out for bad-mouthing the smith's equipment."

Lil threw up her hands. "I was merely showing them how they could increase the heat transfer in their forge with better airflow. Just a simple adjustment in the basin."

"Uninvited," Rek said. "And they sure took it well, too."

Ollahnah raised a hand between them. *"Friend Rek exaggerates. Moohnak was not angered at friend Lil. Though they did feel a little affronted at her suggestions."*

"Let them make the improvements and see how they feel then," Lil said.

"There was no harm done, in any case," Ollahnah said.

Warin laughed, shaking his head.

Something caught Warin's eye to his left. He glanced over just in time to see a large retty emerge from their home, stumbling through one of the posts of their canopy, kicking over assorted stoneware jars and metal utensils on their way with a loud crash. Everyone in the center turned at the noise. The retty did not register anything, their eyes wide and glazed as they gasped like a hiccup, desperately, repeatedly.

They took three steps past the disaster behind them into the open, before falling to the ground with a sickening thud. They did not move again.

Ollahnah raced over to the fallen retty, as did all the other natives in the area, forming a circle of concern around them. Lil, Rek, and Warin stayed by the well. They all were suddenly aware of being apart from the village around them.

Lil touched Warin on the shoulder. "Is it…"

"Yes," Warin said, slowly nodding. "The Bug is here."

By LATE AFTERNOON the sick and dying were everywhere. Rettys lay where they had fallen in the street, too weak to crawl, to even pull themselves along the ground. Others who were not yet afflicted roamed in small groups, picking up the fallen and carrying them, but they were increasingly being outnumbered. Others lay on cots under the canopy of their homes, looking about wildly, reaching for the air randomly as if to pull it toward them. The suddenness of the change in the village was shocking. The vibrant sense of life was gone. Moans and wheezing breaths came from every quarter, filling the void where the sounds of healthy life of just a few hours before seemed to have stopped altogether.

Warin did what he could. As did Lil and Rek. They cared for the natives near them, bringing them water from the well, talking to those who were still conscious, trying to calm them. None but the smallest of the rettys were light enough for the three of them to carry anywhere, but if they could manage it they would at least move them out of the way, to the side of the village path, propping them up against a wall. Ollahnah stayed with them for a time, naming each fallen retty, and then headed off into the village to find their family. For a while they would come back with the fallen retty's loved ones, who would pick them up and take them to their homes. But soon enough the old native would more often come back alone, not saying anything. Shortly before Retti Major fell behind the mountain peaks and the light began to grow dim, Ollahnah left and did not come back.

"We need to go," Rek said to Warin, wiping the sweat from his brow. The two of them stood over a native they had brought to rest underneath the canopy of a home on the edge of the village center.

Warin blinked hard staring at him. "Now?"

Rek took a step closer. "Yes, now. Before it gets dark."

Warin looked around the center. Natives were lying everywhere. Others stumbled along the paths as if in a daze, barely able to keep on their feet. On the far side of the center a large, burly-looking retty fell onto the side of a dome and slid down to the ground. It took him a moment to register that the native looked like Frellanda. He thought of approaching to see, but his feet ignored him.

He looked back at Rek, who stared at him with a fierce practicality.

"We just... abandon them?" he whispered.

"We can't do anything for them," Rek said. "It's too late. We need to get back to the base."

Warin started to speak, but stopped. The fight had drained

out of him and left him without anything to say. Instead he nodded slowly, his eyes downturned.

Rek patted him on the shoulder. "I'm sorry, Warin." Rek tapped his earbud, stepping out into the village center. "I'll contact Bela and Dav, tell them to meet us at the jeep. You get Lil up."

Warin looked and saw Lil, who sat leaning against the side of the first well, her head in her hands. He didn't know when she had sat down. Some time recently, he thought, but he was not sure. He walked up to her and crouched down in front of her.

"Hey," he said. "We're leaving."

Lil didn't move or reply. Warin reached out and touched her shoulder. "Did you hear me?"

Lil looked up at Warin. Her eyes were red, but dry and vacant.

"We're gonna go," Warin said. After a moment, Lil nodded sharply. Warin grabbed her by the shoulders. "Come on, let's get up."

Warin gently lifted Lil off the ground, and she took her own weight on her feet only barely. Warin held on to her by her forearms to keep her from collapsing again. After a moment she brushed his hands away as her feet became more solid. She turned her face away from him, looking down the well behind her.

Rek came walking back up to them. "Are we good to go?" he asked.

"Ready," Warin said. Lil just nodded, not saying anything.

"Bela's already at the jeep waiting for us," Rek said. "But I can't get Dav. He's not answering his comm. We might have to leave without him. I really don't want to be here when the rettys turn on us."

Warin shook his head. "They're not—that's not going to happen."

"You sure?" Rek asked incredulously. "Strangers from another place arrive, and then days later everyone starts dying. They're gonna connect the two eventually."

"No they won't," Warin snapped. "That's us. That's how we would react. They're not like us."

"How can you be so sure?"

"Because I know." Warin closed his eyes, took a deep breath. "Just… get back to the jeep. I'll go get Dav and meet you there."

Rek studied him for a moment, then nodded slowly. "All right. Fine. But don't take too long. I want to be above the fields at least before nightfall."

Rek led Lil away toward the gate. Warin turned and, bracing himself, headed off in the other direction.

Warin weaved in and out of the rettys in the road, careful to stay out of their way. They moved from place to place, some briskly, others more slowly, leaning heavily on each other. Small groups huddled together outside homes around loved ones lying on mats, sometimes the bare ground, wheezing and gasping for breath. Periodic deep, rumbling wails pierced the air both near and far, making him wince. The rettys were so preoccupied they didn't notice him and he felt underfoot.

He wasn't exactly sure where he was going. Vaguely toward the chief's tent in the center, though not directly. He meandered, going up and down roads, circling around, retracing his steps once or twice. It was more a path of least resistance than anything else, turning away from the natives, or at least away from the larger groups of them in the road. He avoided looking around as much as could no matter how contradictory that was to his purpose.

"Wahrin."

Warin turned around. Off to the side of the road he had just walked, Rawilline stood over a table outside a nearby home. The native stared at Warin, their head weaving back and forth.

Warin approached the native. "Have you seen Dav?" he asked them. "I need to find him."

"Friend Dav left," Rawilline replied.

Warin looked surprised. "He left? Left the village?"

"No, just left here. With Edirilla." They pointed over Warin's right shoulder. *"They went in that direction."* Warin glanced in the direction the native pointed. Enough of the headset's camera still covered the native and was able to pick up as Rawilline added, *"In their haste, I do not think they noticed that I did not go with them."*

Warin looked back at Rawilline. He noticed how heavily the native was leaning on the table, both their hands spread wide on its surface. Their eyes were very red, and their body heaved continuously in labored breath.

He stepped closer, putting a hand on the native's forearm. "You're sick," he whispered.

"I am not alone," they replied, gesturing to a figure on the ground nearby.

"I'll find Edirilla and bring them back here. With the healer." Warin started to turn away. "I'll be right back."

Rawilline grabbed his arm. *"No, friend Warin, it is all right. They have many things to fret about without me. Someone will come for me soon enough."* The native paused, then said, *"You need to leave."*

Warin shook his head. "I need to find Dav."

"Friend Dav does not want to be found by you," Rawilline said. *"He knew where you were. We saw you in the village center before and he stayed with us."*

"He's going to stay?"

"He ignored me when I told him to go. Many times." Rawilline coughed. *"Friend Dav is quite stubborn."*

Warin was silent for a long time, then said, "I could stay too. I could help. I said I would."

"Can you?" Rawilline asked. Warin said nothing and they continued. *"Many in the village have already gone back to the fields today, friend Warin. I fear many more will go tomorrow. Even if I am not among those, I will be following soon. Can you truly help us?"*

Warin looked around. A young retty pulled a two-wheeled cart along the road, its bulky contents covered by a blanket. An infant crawled over the torso of their wheezing parent sitting against the side of a wall, oblivious to the world.

Warin closed his eyes, suddenly heavy with water. "I wanted to. There just wasn't time."

"Then go, friend Warin, and spare yourself. You do not need this burden." Rawilline looked up at the sky. It was just beginning to darken, and here and there greater stars were starting to flash. *"I would have liked to have seen the other worlds. Seen yours, friend Warin. Met all the others you said there were."*

"They would have liked to meet you too," Warin said, his voice cracking.

Rawilline's head dropped, suddenly very heavy. *"You will have to give them all my greetings."*

Warin nodded, taking a long, stuttered breath. He muted his headset and stretched out his hands, palms facing forward. "Rawilline. Joolid," he said.

Rawilline reached across the table slowly, their arm shaking, and grasped Warin's right hand. The native shook it very slowly. "Wahrin. Joolid," they whispered.

The native let go of his hand and slouched down deep onto the table, their legs buckling into a kneeling position beneath them. They cradled their head on their forearm. All three of their eyes closed in unison.

Thirteen

WARIN STOOD IN the dark at the windows of the operations deck, staring out into the night. The clouds were thick above, blocking out the stars, so the valley was in total darkness—the outline of the mountains across the valley were barely visible. There was one faint light, barely a pinprick in the black, down where the village was. It was too far away to be the light from a home, so an outdoor campfire, perhaps. He could have opened an infrared and magnified window in the smart glass and seen the village just fine. But he didn't.

During the day he did. Even though at the maximum magnification, the village looked calm, very still, not all that different than it had always looked before. There were no raging fires or collapsing buildings, any signs of the chaos and death that he knew were going on, that he imagined as he stared. But from this distance, far removed from it all, the only difference he actually saw was the lack of gray smudges. The natives moving about the village. There were fewer and fewer of them each day. And the numerous dark dots that were slowly filling up fields. The dark overturned soil of newly dug graves.

He was alone on the deck. Gare was closed off in her office as she had been all day, and Lil—she hadn't left her room since they had returned from the village. She must leave sometime, if for no other reason than to get food. But he hadn't seen her, and he was sure Gare and Rek hadn't either. They would have mentioned it. And there was no way she would want to see Bela.

The ride back in the jeep had been hard. And Bela hadn't made it any easier. "I guess the mission of mercy is off now, huh?" she said with a smirk from the back seat. She tapped Warin sitting next to her on the shoulder. "You still want me to show you how to make a vaccine?"

Warin said nothing, clenching his jaw shut. Bela continued. "Mind you, a vaccine wouldn't have done any good. You could have saved the village and everyone in it, sure. But then all their future children would die because they weren't vaccinated against the Bug because they didn't exist yet when you were inoculating everyone. Were you planning on somehow getting the Ministry to let you stick around and keep violating policy, over and over? Or were you going to develop an airborne anti-viral to wipe out the bug planet-wide too? How long were you planning on staying here?"

"At least he wanted to try," Lil said coldly. "At least we care."

Bela stared at the back of Lil's head for a moment. Warin could see her grind her teeth. "Oh, you sure do care," she said. "Your petition. All those documents you were going to leak. The uproar you were going to cause on the net amongst the influencers. That'll fix things. Hell, it might have gone viral. Nothing helps like millions of people publicly wringing their hands."

Bela smiled wickedly at Lil, who wouldn't turn around, tried to pretend she wasn't there, hadn't said anything. But Bela wasn't finished. She leaned forward on the back of the front seat. "There's still time, you know, if you really want to do your white savior routine and save the noble savages. After the village is wiped out, there's still going to be what, five hundred, maybe a thousand rettys left on the planet who survived the Bug? No plague is perfect. Most of them will be dead soon too, though. No group safety keeping predators away, inadequate understanding or skills for farming—or foraging. And of course mishaps, accidents, or other illnesses that they can't survive without help. One of those will get most of them before winter."

"Shut up," Lil said, her voice shaking.

Bela ignored her and continued. "I suppose some of them will manage to avoid those fates and survive long-term. Maybe a handful. But they will be so spread out planetwide that they'll never see another of their kind, so they'll never have children and die alone in thirty, forty years."

"That's enough, Bela," Rek said forcefully.

Bela ignored him too and kept going. "But no, listen, maybe you can get the Ministry to collect up all the surviving rettys and concentrate them someplace nice. In a camp. There they can live happily ever after on their reservation, out of the way of the mining and cattle-farm settlements we'll be putting down everywhere else, as the birth defects that come from inadequate genetic diversity and inbreeding make them weaker and sicker, each generation worse than the last. They could probably last two hundred years that way. Three hundred, even. But definitely no longer than that. But hey, that's better than nothing, right? You'll still get to pretend you did something good for them."

"I said that's enough!" Rek shouted, turning around from the front seat.

"Is it?" Bela replied just as loudly. "I've had to listen to it from her for months. Ever since she first noticed what I knew was happening two years ago. Where were you back then? Where were any of you? Tell me I don't care. If I had tried to do something back when it might have made a difference, would any of you have helped? Would you, Lil, or are petitions the limit of your dedication?" Bela turned to look at Warin. "You wouldn't have; you didn't care until after your field trip. 'It's so depressing,' remember? And Rek, you don't even care now." Bela sat back, spent. "Don't any of you *ever* tell me what I care about."

For the rest of the ride back, Lil stared ahead blankly, like an automaton waiting to be switched on. Nobody spoke to her— nobody spoke at all. Warin could see in the faint reflection of her face in the windshield the dark cloud that had come over her, hinting at the dark thoughts that must be going through her head. She barely waited for the jeep to come to a full stop in the base garage before she was out the door.

"Bela was way out of line," Rek had said to Warin the next day in the galley. "Lil may be a little pompous and self-righteous, and it's not like she didn't say shit about the rest of us all the time, but there was no need for that."

Warin said nothing, nodding into his food. Rek continued. "And I do care. Just as much as anyone else. I know what a tragedy this all is. It's just..." Rek leaned in closer across the table. "Do you remember that figurine? The one you had at your camp?"

Warin looked up over Rek's head, remembering how the statue reflected the firelight.

"You remember I took a scan of it?" he asked Warin. "Well, I compared it to some other artifacts that have been collected over the years. From an ancient settlement on Llama—"

"Gregan," Warin said.

Rek started. "What?"

Warin glared at Rek. "The continent's called Gregan."

"By who?"

"By them."

Rek nodded. "Gregan. Okay, fine." Warin leaned down into

his food again. Rek continued. "Anyway, there's this old village there that was buried in a volcanic eruption some twelve thousand years ago. Just completely buried. And perfectly preserved. Like Pompeii and Herculaneum back on Earth. It's been a helluva resource. We've found many figurines and other sculptures like yours there. And I mean a lot like yours. I analyzed the scans I took of your piece and compared it to some of those artifacts. They could have been carved by the same artist, they are so alike. Same style, identical technique."

Warin glanced up at him. "You're an archaeologist now?"

Rek straightened in his seat. "I dabble in it. It overlaps with geology. Anyway, I talked with a friend back at the Ministry's artifacts section who is an archaeologist, and they agree with me. Your figurine is exactly like those from the destroyed village. You realize what that means?"

Warin barely shook his head.

Rek tilted his head down, trying to make eye contact with Warin. "It means the rettys are exactly the same as they were the day that village got buried in ash twelve thousand years ago. And it's not just the art. The tools we find are the same, the homes, the layout of the fields, it's all just like it is down in the valley. They have not evolved or improved anything in that whole time. Twelve thousand years, Warin, with no meaningful societal advancement. That's almost twice as long as our entire recorded history. And it's likely been even longer than that since the rettys had any kind of meaningful civilizational progress. And before you even think it, there's nothing that suggests any kind of worldwide societal collapse in between that they were recovering from, either. They just never kept advancing. They were too comfortable where they were, so they stagnated.

"A civilization only gets a small window to build up in before something comes along that tries to wipe them out—an ice age, a caldera eruption, a major asteroid strike. A pandemic like the Bug. Any one of those—it's just a matter of time on any planet. Great filters, Warin. We had them. We almost didn't make it through the ice age at the beginning, plagues nearly got us at least twice, we nearly blew ourselves up, and then right after that we nearly made the Earth uninhabitable. But we survived and kept going. Because we kept advancing. Getting better. Better tools, better technology, better understanding. The rettys didn't do any of that. It's just not the way they're wired. Their minds never developed the drive or the ambition to improve, because they never needed it. When they were evolving they didn't have enough conflict with nature to push them enough; they just grew too big to challenge. So when they became the dominant life on the planet, the civilization they created was a passive one. One with practically no aggression. You know, I don't think they've ever had anything you or I would consider a war anywhere on the planet?"

Rek paused, expecting Warin to speak. When he saw no reply was coming, he continued. "And look: I know that sounds nice, but without the conflicts between groups there was even less to motivate them to keep advancing. No need to build walls, or weapons, so no need for advanced engineering. No need for allies, or treaties, so no need for advancement in political science, or the philosophies behind it. The rettys just got themselves to a place of relative comfort and stopped. The same place they were thousands of years ago, and where they would likely have been thousands of years from now. Maybe they would have progressed sooner or later, but a natural filter got them first. They weren't fast enough."

Rek swirled the cup in his hand for a moment. He looked up at Warin with a forced shrug. "This whole thing, it's tragic, Warin. But it was inevitable."

Warin said nothing, giving Rek no indication that he was listening. And he hadn't wanted to hear any of it. Yet every time their paths crossed since they got back, when Warin sat for a meal, or at his station, or at the window staring down into the valley, Rek would start in on the rettys' fatal flaws, how nothing could have been done. That it was all so inevitable. It never varied much in content or in Rek's insistence on it all. Warin would just let him talk, barely engaging with him, but also not bothering to tell him to shut up or go away. Eventually he would leave on his own. Rek's rationalization was all just so much buzzing in his ear, barely getting through the heavy blandness Warin had been in since the village. None of it mattered to him. The only thing in any of Rek's lectures that made any impression on him at all was thinking about the figurine that he had left in the village when they fled.

The spot of light in the blackness out the window slowly faded out, making the sense of void and nothingness in the valley past the glass absolute.

"Come in."

Warin stepped through the doorway to Gare's office and it slid closed behind him. She gestured at the seat on the other side of her desk and Warin sat down.

Gare stared at her holopad a long time before speaking. A 2D form hovered in the air between them. It was fuzzy from his vantage but he recognized the layout of a report. She looked up at Warin. "I still haven't been able to make contact with Dav. He hasn't reported in since the Bug hit the village. Has he been filing reports with you?"

Warin shook his head. "I haven't gotten anything from him either."

"And you haven't tried to contact him yourself?"

"No," Warin said. The idea of trying hadn't even occurred to him.

Gare shook her head with a sigh. "Dav," she muttered. "I knew he was too close to them. All the years he's been on this planet studying the rettys. It'll be fifteen years next fall. Of course he grew too attached, lost his impartiality about them. Half the reason I sent you down there with Dav was I hoped you'd have a focusing influence on him."

"Because you thought I didn't care?" Warin asked her.

"No," Gare replied quickly. "That's not what I meant. Of course you care. We all care about what's happened to the rettys. But you weren't as invested in them as he was. You had some distance and could help him keep things in perspective."

"And what perspective is that?"

"That we are only researchers. We don't play God with our subjects. We don't get to decide their future."

"Or whether they have one or not."

Gare grimaced. "Beings die every day, Warin. Whole species, just like the rettys. Hell, somewhere in the universe one or two have probably died off since you sat down. Nobody did anything to help them, either. The rettys aren't the first extinction we've witnessed and they won't be the last. And every time it's just as tragic. But we can't become the arbiters of life and death in the galaxy, Warin. It's not our job."

Warin nodded slowly but didn't reply.

Gare continued. "I am sorry for sending you down to the village. It was not my smartest decision. I thought you would help Dav. Beyond that, I honestly thought I was doing you a favor."

"I know," Warin said. "Time in the field looks good on the record."

"Well, it does. You can't get ahead if you don't show an ability to be adaptable. I think you have a really bright future with the Ministry. And I bet there's going to be an even greater need for administrators soon."

"There will?"

Gare smiled. "They haven't been released yet, but I've seen the reports on the next generation of starship drives from the Ministry. They've had a major breakthrough with them. They're a tenfold increase in energy output from our best current engines."

Warin raised his eyebrows. "That much?"

"At least. Which means a tenfold increase in operational range. When the new ships come floating out of the docks in a few years, we'll have at least three more sectors in the Orion Arm within our range. With thousands of new systems to explore. We're about to have another expansion boom. Possibly the biggest one we've ever had."

Warin sat back in his seat, thinking.

"But still, if I had known how it would end in the valley… I feel responsible for what you had to see down there."

"It's all right," Warin replied with a tight smile. "You didn't know."

Gare nodded furrowing her brow. "I probably should have, though." She sat back in her seat, crossing her arms across her chest. "That being said, you really should have tried harder to bring Dav back with you."

Warin shook his head. "I don't think anything short of hogtying him and dragging him by his feet would have worked. Besides, I couldn't find him to even try."

"Yes, I read your report," Gare said with a deep sigh. "It really does not look good, him being out there out of contact with base this long."

"He's fine," Warin said. "I saw him in the village just yesterday. Well, what I think was him. It's hard to tell at this distance."

"I've seen him too. That's why I've put off writing him up. Or sending anyone down to get him. Which wouldn't look good for me but would generate unflattering paperwork on him as well. But everybody is dealing with a lot right now, so…" Gare shook herself and sat forward. "Eh, it's not your problem anyway. There's another thing I needed to talk to you about."

Gare waved a finger above her holopad, closing the report and bringing up another document. She turned it in the air to face Warin. He leaned forward to read it.

It was his transfer request. It had been approved.

"It's effective immediately," Gare said. "*Ignacio* docked at the orbital station last night, and there's a cabin with your name on it."

Warin looked at Gare. "What about my replacement?"

"I can handle your job short-term till they send someone," she said. "Not that there's much to it right now. It's going to be pretty quiet around here for a little while. The Ministry is likely going to replace everyone now that the Retii mission priorities will be changing. Rek will probably stay. Bela maybe, but I doubt it. Dav will go if he ever comes back. And Lil definitely needs a change of scenery. I put in a rush transfer order for her this morning. I hope I can get her on *Ignacio* with you. Honestly, the sooner she gets somewhere else, the better for everyone. I might get rotated out myself eventually. You're only first because your transfer was already in the works."

"So," Warin said, softly. "That's it."

Gare nodded. "That's it. Your assignment on Retti 4 is officially over. You could head up to the launchpad, fly a shuttle up to the orbital station, and board the freighter the moment you leave this office."

Warin didn't say anything, staring at Gare with his mouth

open. Gare furrowed her brow at him. "This is what you wanted, correct?" she asked.

"Well, yeah. It is," he stammered. "It's just that I completely forgot about it."

"Well, it didn't forget about you." Gare leaned forward on her elbows on her desk. "You've been a good station manager, Warin, your work is always exemplary. It's been a pleasure. You should get a pretty good new assignment. This whole thing about Dav, don't worry about it, it's not your fault. It won't reflect badly on you, I'll make sure of it."

"I appreciate that," Warin said, shaking his head, thinking.

Gare stood up from her seat. "We're going to need people like you, Warin, in the coming years. Young, ambitious, capable people. We've only just begun to explore. And somewhere out there is a spot for you on my side of this desk. And it's not as many years away as you might think."

On his way back to his quarters, his finger paused in the elevator as he stared at the button for the launchpad on top of the base. He really could just punch that button and leave, just like Gare had said. Spend his time on the cruiser relaxing, away from all the morose air and tension down here. She'd said a cabin for him, right? They might mean an officer's quarters, with space, a window, and his own food dispenser. But even a crowded berth with the crew would be fine, better even, being around life, other people with things to talk and think about besides this planet. And then, in a few days, a week, maybe two, he would be gone. Out of the system. Never to return.

He pressed the button for the living quarters.

He didn't have much he needed to pack. Nothing, really. Most of his things he could possibly need were still down at his campsite in the village. Maybe grab a snack or two, just in case. He doubted he'd need the headset, but he grabbed it off his desk anyway, along with his pouch of oxygen tablets. He opened it and looked inside. There were only four tablets left. He had gotten pretty well acclimated to the atmosphere in his time in the village—by the end he only needed one, maybe two of them a day. So those few would likely be enough. Even so, to be safe he decided he'd fill the pouch up on the way out tomorrow morning.

Fourteen

THE EARLY-MORNING mist was a little over knee-high as Warin approached the village entrance. The suns had not yet risen above the peaks in the east to evaporate it, leaving the valley itself still in the foggy shade of imminent dawn, even as the sky above was morning-bright. It gave everything a dull sheen as if being viewed through a filter.

He had parked the jeep around the bend in the road out of sight of the village and decided to walk in on foot. There was no reason he couldn't have driven right up to the entrance—no reason he couldn't have driven in and through the village itself. But the idea of doing that made him uncomfortable. So he left the vehicle behind and walked in with a grim stride.

As he got closer, he glanced up at the hills on both sides of the path. He saw no natives up there looking down on him. Or the small dark figures in groups of two or three in the fields watching. There was no group of rettys trailing behind him on the road, either. As he came over the small rise to the plateau, he saw the village entrance ahead, indistinct and blurry in the fog, but there. No one waited for him as they had done when he had first come to the village. He walked through the entrance, keeping to the center of the road. He did not dare enter any of the homes.

Everything was as it was when he had fled days before with

the others. There were no ruined structures or corpses in the street. No scorch marks from smoldering fires, dark stains of blood on the walls or ground, any signs of chaos. Mostly he saw abandoned bowls of food, half-folded blankets, or a carelessly dropped tool outside a home. He passed by a table that had overturned, spilling its contents onto the ground. The edge of the table had half-split a large vase as it fell like a knife stuck into a stick of butter. But beyond minor things like that, there was nothing. If he hadn't known what had happened here, he would have been hard pressed to find any clue of it. There was no destruction, no death in the air. Just absence.

The stillness of everything was overwhelming. The silence. He remembered how unnerved he had felt at the quiet when he had first came to the village, but it was nothing compared to this. As quiet as it had been before, there was always something, a thousand little sounds, the squeak of cartwheels, the grating of sandpaper against wood, the grunts and squeals of people at work and play. Of all the life going on. But now there was nothing at all. And the silence was so absolute it pressed on his ears. So much so that when he heard the echoed ping of something metal hitting cobblestone a few roads away, the slight noise made him jump.

He found Dav sitting on a log with a native outside a home near the northern fence, next to a hastily dug fire pit in the ground by the road. It had long since gone to ash, with only a wisp of smoke floating up from it. The pair of them looked weary beyond measure. Dav rested heavily on his arms propped on his knees, his canteen dangling from the fingers of his hand as if it could fall at any moment. The retty sat on the ground next to him, their head slightly unsteady on their shoulders, looking emaciated, their eyes bleary and red. Both of them were disheveled, their clothing frayed and covered in dark stains. As Warin approached they both looked up at him in unison, their faces blank, too weary for emotion.

Warin stood before them, not sure what to say. After a time, Dav smirked at him.

"Welcome back," he said dryly.

Warin stepped closer. "Dav—"

Dav put up a hand. "Only a joke," he said. "Gallows humor. You were smart to leave when you did."

Warin looked around. "Is everyone…"

Dav nodded. "Everyone. Well, except for Helluna here." Dav turned to the native. "Say hello to the only native retty left in the village. Probably the only one in over a hundred kilometers in any direction. As of yesterday."

Warin stared at the native, who turned to look back up at him evenly. They blinked their eyes at him in unison. They were young, by his best guess just short of a full adult, though their slim arms and neck might have influenced that judgment. Their hair was short, shaved almost down to the skin on their necks and arms, with spots of dark color. Warin couldn't tell if it was dye or grime.

Warin extended his hands, palms outward to Helluna. "Helluna. Joolid," he said softly.

The entire village, all those natives. Now just this one alone…

Helluna bobbed their head at him wearily. "Wahrin," the native said slowly. "Joolid." They then continued with several grunts and other sounds. Warin grabbed for his headset tucked into his belt, but by the time he had it in his hands the native had stopped talking. They stood slowly, very wearily, and walked off, putting a hand gently on Dav's shoulder as they did.

"What did they say?" Warin asked Dav, stuffing the headset back into his belt.

Dav sighed. "They asked if you have come to take me home now that the work is done." He coughed lightly. "It's not actually done. There are still a few more that need to be buried. Ten, maybe twenty. But Helluna thinks I've done enough and worries I'll keel over if I stay."

"You look like you might."

Dav laughed weakly and took a sip from his canteen.

Warin dragged a nearby stump over next to him and sat down. "Gare's pretty upset with you," he said.

"For staying?"

"And not reporting in."

"If I had reported in, she would have ordered me to leave."

"True," Warin said. "She hasn't written you up yet, though. There's still nothing official in your record."

"That's very considerate of her," Dav said. "I bet she's kicking herself for letting me visit in the first place." He offered his canteen to Warin, who politely refused. Dav stared off at the distant mountains near where the observation post was. "The first day was the worst. Half the village seemed to fall ill, but only about fifty or so died that first night. But it was the suddenness of it. The shock. All the rettys falling in such a short time, almost as if it was timed that way. I knew the Bug worked fast, all the reports said so, but you really can't appreciate just how fast until you see it up close." Dav snapped his fingers. "Like that. One moment they were fine, and then the next… You must have seen some of that."

Warin thought of Rawilline, leaning on the table. "I did."

Dav closed his eyes, nodding. "More than one hundred fifty died the next day. It was in full swing. The healer had been so frantic, rushing from place to place to treat them all. Or trying to. Deep down I think they knew it was hopeless. It was, after all. Everyone by that point had already been infected and it was just a matter of time. But the healer kept at it anyway. Trying different herbs, salves on the torso, inhaling smokes, anything thing they could think of. Right up until they died themself. On day three, I think. Or maybe it was day four. It was the day after Edirilla went. Pointless, really."

"Dav—"

Dav kept going. "You know, it wasn't as bad as you might think," he said. "I mean, it was horrible, watching a whole village of nearly eight hundred rettys get wiped out, watching them as they all knew they were doomed, but there wasn't any of the nightmarish chaos that you would get in humans in their situation. No rioting, or looting, burning, no violent attacks on one another. Nobody even fled as far as I know. There was a lot of sadness and a lot of fear, of course, it was so thick you could barely walk through it at times. But not the societal decay. It's strange. To the very end they remained civilized. Kept their dignity. Almost accepting of their fate. Maybe they were too intent on making sure that every one of them got into the ground to even consider destruction."

"Every one of them was buried?"

"Every one of them," Dav answered. "It was all we've done for the last few days. Bring the dead out to the field, dig a hole for them, and 'plant them.' That's what they call it. They're not very deep graves, barely over a meter and a half. Deep enough to keep scavengers from catching their scent at least. The soil is very soft. And before you fill them in, you say 'Ivva don nara tooloon.' Roughly translated, 'Now you will feed your children'. Except their children were likely in the hole next to them." Dav laughed shortly, rolling his neck counterclockwise. "We filled up Inna field and most of the one next to it, Uvva, I think it's called."

"The whole village between the two of you?"

Dav shook his head at Warin. "I only dug six myself. I don't have the strength of the rettys. I'm too old. I helped carry them out from their homes more. Pushing the cart. Everyone still alive in the village was either with a cart like me or digging. Until they fell too. It was literally all that mattered to them in the end. You remember Tyundelorro? The scavenger? They must have dug over a hundred graves on their own. Literally right up to their last moment, too. Every time I came back with a new load of the dead to be buried, I saw them out in the field, digging. For days I saw them out there. I don't know if they ever took a break. Others around them would weaken and stop, come to the fence to lay down to die, but they just kept going. Tyundelorro was one of the last standing. Then the day before last, I came back and I didn't see them. Turns out, when Tyundelorro felt the Bug start to get them, they dug one more grave, laid their shovel aside, removed their tunic, and crawled in. That's where we found them."

Dav took a drink of water and spit it into the fire pit. It hissed faintly. Warin glanced down into the fire pit and spotted the remains of a blue, ornately woven sleeve of a native's tunic. Then half the white collar of another, simpler one. And then another, a long strip of fabric, a blackened hem, in which he could see white trim. Like Rawilline's or Edirilla's.

He looked back to Dav, who watched him with a smirk. "No casket, no shroud, nothing but them. They go into the ground as they came into the world. It's a fairly romantic sentiment, don't you think? Or it's just a way to keep the dyes in the fabric from affecting the crop."

Dav was silent for a long time. He rubbed at his eyes heavily to wake up, smudging the thick dirt stains on his cheeks. Warin watched him quietly.

"You know, I'll have a helluva report out of all of this," he finally said. "More than one, actually. There are so many different topics I've learned about in my time with them. Nobody has ever interacted with them before, not like I have. Makes me the preeminent expert on the rettys. Just think how much I can tell people about their attitude towards death alone."

Warin reached out and put a hand on his shoulder. Dav looked at him. "I always liked to imagine, some day thousands of years from now, long after I'm gone and forgotten, that the descendants of these rettys would make it out to space. And we'd meet them, and welcome them into the interstellar community. When we did, we'd share with them all the research we had done on them as they developed. I liked to imagine how surprised they would be to read it, maybe learn things about themselves at this time in their history that even they had no idea about. The idea tickled me. Can you imagine how they'd react? And there'd be my name at the very top. They'd wonder about what kind of a person I was, contemplate my conclusions about them. Such a strange kind of immortality." Dav took a long drink from his canteen, and then dropped it on the ground. "But that's all over now. There's no future. And all I've researched about them, written about them, it'll be filed away in the database and eventually forgotten."

Dav stood up and walked away, off in the direction that Helluna had gone.

Fifteen

WARIN'S CAMPSITE IN the grove was exactly as he had left it. His tent set up on the edge of the small clearing in the trees, the tent flap only half-closed, the tail of it waving gently in an unfelt breeze. Lil and Rek's packs laid on the ground beside it. Next to the entrance a few odds and ends were left out, a folding shovel stuck into the dirt, a flashlight resting next to it, one of his shirts draped across a tree-stump stool he had borrowed from the neighborhood well for sitting on. And on top of the shirt the dark figurine sat, where Rek had placed it after taking his scan. He smiled lightly. If he had known he would be gone so long, he would have tidied up.

Warin picked up the figurine and sat down in its place. It had a light dusting of purplish pollen on it that stood out starkly on the black stone. He wiped it off the figurine's face with his thumb, staring into the tiny oval of its central eye. There was no detail inside of it, but the light reflected in a small ball of white in the eye that gave the impression of a pupil. It followed him as he turned the figurine in his hand. He smiled. To hear Rek describe it, you would think the style rustic, primitive almost, but it wasn't. He thought it was a very sophisticated work, with the smooth curves of line and symmetry of the body and the intricacy of the braided hair along the neck and arms. You could feel the friendliness exuding from that face—even a hint of the world-weariness from a life spent wandering. It was advanced enough.

Enaa the Traveller. He never did get to hear the stories about them. Or any of the founders. He had meant to, sooner or later. Ollahnah would have enjoyed telling him the tales, might have made a whole thing about it, spending an entire day regaling him with the tales of the founding of the village. Perhaps it was the level of enthusiasm that he knew Ollahnah would have had that made him never ask. But now he wished he had. Too late. He was sure Dav had meticulous notes on them all. Maybe he even recorded someone telling them. But that wouldn't be the same.

A strong gust of wind whipped through the grove, making the trees hiss, the branches groan and crack. Leaves and other small debris flew in a whirl between the trees and then floated back down to the ground again as the wind abated. A single leaf landed on the torso of the figurine in his hand, stuck between the arm and the staff it held.

Warin picked the leaf out of the figurine. This was the special delicacy he had seen the rettys chew on. He had never actually looked at one that closely. It was circular and blue, darker on the front and lighter on the underside, with white veins leading up through it from the stem. He rubbed it between his fingers. It was very springy, more than he would have expected it to be. It bent in between his thumb and first finger halfway before he felt any further would snap it in two. When he opened his fingers it bounced back flat instantly. He brought it up to his nose and smelled it. It had a faint evergreen odor, not unlike mouthwash. He twirled it in his hands a few times. The leaf looked healthy and clean.

He tapped it quickly against his tongue. Then did so again for a fraction longer. A little tingle of sour prickled where the leaf had touched. What he had tried of the rettys' food had been somewhat bland, or if anything sweet like the unna roots. So the sourness of the leaf was somewhat of a surprise. He rolled his tongue around inside his mouth, spreading the faint taste further. His cheeks puckered slightly.

He took a deep breath and, in one quick motion, popped the leaf into his mouth and closed his lips tight. After a moment of it resting on his tongue, he slowly ground it between his teeth.

And violently spit the leaf back out.

When his teeth shredded the leaf the sourness of it was over-whelming. The whole inside of his mouth clenched stiff with it. And it was coupled with a gritty taste of mud that turned his saliva thick as molasses. He grabbed for his canteen and rinsed his mouth out, spitting it off to his side. He repeated it several times until he ran out of water. But he couldn't completely get the taste out of his mouth.

"An acquired taste, I guess," he mumbled to himself, spitting.

Warin put the figurine down on the ground. He should get started packing up his things. No point in delaying. He unzipped the tent flap, kneeled down, and stuck his head inside. There were a few random bits of clothing around his air mattress against the far side of the tent, and his own hardcase pack resting on its side next to it, its top open. His pistol and holster rested on the ground by the pack.

He crawled farther into the tent and turned his mattress over, which was cumbersome in the enclosed space. He flipped the small motor on the back of the mattress in reverse and turned it on. The motor whined and the mattress deflated with a gasp-ing sound as it folded in on itself. As that worked he started stuffing things inside his pack, pushing down on them to make them fit. The taste in his mouth grew strong for a moment, and he winced, swallowing, sending it down his throat. He could feel it spread out like lines into his lungs, his chest, his arms. And it throbbed slightly.

"An acquired taste, I guess," he mumbled to himself again.

He turned around on his knees and was surprised to see the mattress was gone. Where it had been only a moment ago was just the empty corner of the tent. It had been there; he was sure of it. Where had it gone? He bent down and looked at the place where it had been carefully for any sign of it. It had to be around here somewhere. He could still hear it deflating.

No, he had packed it already. He looked in his pack. Yes, there it was. The edge of it sticking out from underneath a shirt.

But he still heard the mattress deflating.

Warin exited the tent, dragging his pack behind him, and sat down heavily, his back against the stump stool. His mouth was so thick that he could not get his tongue off the roof of his mouth. The taste had gone, at least. It had moved on from his mouth and chest and was now in his fingers, which felt soft. He pressed his thumb to his fingers, one after another as hard as he could, but barely felt anything at all.

How long had he been doing that for?

Warin shook his head. He needed to focus. This was all the leaf. It was messing with his head.

He looked down at the figurine by his knee. "This explains why the grove was so popular," he said to it.

The figurine smiled up at him from the ground, but didn't say a word. He couldn't be sure, but he thought it looked a little exasperated. He covered the figurine with his foot to make it stop looking at him.

He was vaguely aware of the state he was in. Or at least he occasionally would remember. But then he'd lose himself trying to remember if the trees were supposed to be green or the sky white. The leaves were definitely blue, yes, he was sure that was right. But what about the smell of roses in the air? Had it always smelled like that? There weren't any roses on this planet. And that couldn't possibly be a robin in the tree branch above him. He couldn't see it, but it sure sounded like one. He thought about it. No, of course there was no bird. It had to be a distortion, a strange echo of the sound of his mattress deflating.

Warin shook his head sharply. He'd lost himself again. He took several long deep breaths to try and gain his wits. What a sorry sight he must be, he thought, flopped on the ground, his head bobbing around as if it was on a swivel. Embarrassing. There was no one around to see him like this, thankfully. Also thankfully he hadn't tried a leaf before now. That wouldn't have gone well. He could just imagine Rawilline coming to visit him as they had that one time, only to find him like this. His pupils were probably as big as saucers. No way Rawilline would have failed to notice. They probably would have been diplomatic about it. But *he'd still know*. Warin could see them standing there, looking down at him as he rolled around and talked gibberish, shaking their head at him.

"Don't look at me like that," he said to them. "They're your trees."

Rawilline didn't reply. They didn't move at all.

Wait. No, of course they didn't say anything. They weren't here. Right. Yes, Rawilline was gone. He closed his eyes. Immediately up and down left him. Only when he opened them again did he get perspective back. He decided not to do that again if he could help it. And there was no Rawilline in front of him anymore. Except they had never been there to begin with, he had just imagined his friend standing there seeing him in this state. His friend? Yes, his friend.

He wished they were here.

Warin rubbed his scalp and face in his hands. The damn leaf. He needed to focus, ride it out. It couldn't last forever. Could it? No, of course not. He hoped. The uncertainty of it made him panic a little. Imagine being like this for the rest of his life. Which wouldn't be long out here in the wilderness, with nothing but rotting food and more leaves to eat. He'd never make it back to the base. He doubted he could even make it out of the village. Stuck here forever, listening to that damn mattress deflating.

"Calm down, calm down," he mumbled to himself. "It won't last forever. That's just crazy. It'll pass." The words helped a little. He had forgotten what he had been panicking about, which helped more.

He picked up his canteen from the ground where he had dropped it. He needed water to flush his system out. He needed to get to the well.

He had great trouble finding the path out of the grove. It should have been just a few rows of trees over from his camp, where it had always been, but the path he found there didn't look like the right one. He turned around, thinking he had somehow missed it. But he only wound up back at his camp again. The figurine practically laughed at him. Maybe he had headed off in the wrong direction. He thought that was entirely possible. He set out again in the opposite direction from before. But there was no path at all that way. Just more trees. When he saw the village border fence he turned back around, because that was definitely not the right direction. He didn't want to see the fields on the other side of it. He hoped to get back to his camp, regain his bearings, and try another direction. But now he couldn't find it. He turned and walked in a different direction for a while. Then turned again. But the most he could do was find himself near the village fence again where he would turn and hurry away. He started to feel frustrated. The grove couldn't possibly be this big.

After some time he found the path. It still did not look like the right one, but at least it wasn't the fence again. He sat down heavily by the side of it. He kept shifting his seat, as the pins and needles in the ground kept jabbing him, irritating his backside. He tried to open his mouth but his lips had dried shut. They wouldn't separate. He could feel the sour taste in his toes now. He wiggled them and watched the surface of his boots to see if it was visible.

He slapped at something stinging him on his arm. The sound of the slap and the sting roused him and he looked up from his feet. The trees around him were very dark, the black between their trunks looking like a solid void. How long had he been sitting there? He looked up through the trees. The sky was noticeably darker. Was it dark like that when he had sat down? He couldn't remember.

Water. He still needed water.

He looked down the path, to his right and to his left. Which way led to the well? He was sure only one direction did.

Warin stood up. That shadow down the path to the right looked like it knew where it was going.

He followed the shadow as it jumped about in the trees on both sides of him. Though he stayed on the path, not feeling the need to follow its exact steps. At points he had to stop to clear his head, as the sound of the mattress deflating grew piercing in his ears. Fortunately the shadow seemed to wait for him when he did and only continued on when he was ready.

Finally the trees went away, just before total night fell on him. It was more bearable in the open space between the native structures. The feel of the cobblestones on his feet through his shoes was a welcome sensation.

He hurried his pace, feeling more certain of himself now, and more desperate to relieve his thirst. His mouth felt like one solid block of mud. He barely acknowledged the greetings from the natives by their homes and on the road as he passed by. They weren't really there, he didn't actually see them. More just the impression of them. Their memory. Somehow he knew that. But he still felt bad not greeting them as he passed. He would go back after he got some water.

Warin fell into the side of the well, grasping the edge of it in his hands. He looked over the side, into the void of darkness beneath. Somewhere down there was the water. He hoped. It looked so impossibly empty of anything, such a complete and total black that it seemed insane to think anything could come out of it. It was the kind of dark that only took things, nothing ever returned from it. Was there really water down there? But he had gotten water from it before, though. Yes, he had, he remembered doing so many times. Of course there was water down there.

He untied the rope from the side and the bucket dropped down into the void with a whoosh, disappearing instantly. He thought he heard a splash but he also thought he might have imagined it. He stared down for a long time, uncertain. No way to tell if the bucket had reached the water yet. He pulled on the rope and it seemed heavier than it should be. He let the rope go again, and far down below the bucket hit the water with an echoed splash. Yes. That time he was sure he heard it. He pulled the bucket back up quickly, reaching out to grab it below him when it was barely a vague something at the edge of the dark.

Warin poured the bucket over his face. The water from the well was ice-cold and fresh, and immediately the caked mud in his mouth dissolved, and he opened his lips and filled his throat. His head began to clear. He sat down against the well, drenched, as his body relaxed, and the sour taste finally seemed to fade from his body.

"One of you could have warned me about the leaves," he said, laughing.

The impressions of the natives nearby glanced at him but said nothing.

Warin held out his hand in front of his face, turning it over and back. He made a fist. His fingers still felt very soft—all of him did, actually. But the sense of panic and confusion was gone. The effect seemed to have settled. He felt very calm, more in tune with the nighttime world around him. It was all somewhat blurry, covered in some kind of mist maybe, but he saw the homes, the cobblestones, the impressions of the rettys standing around him well enough.

He watched as their impressions passed by him, or milled about nearby talking in small groups. They weren't really here anymore. He knew that. Or mostly still knew that. But the oft-repeated pattern of their lives were burned into the world.

Some were unfamiliar to him. A native sitting by their home weaving flax. Children running in circles around the adults. Others he recognized. Frellanda rushing by, late for the fields, their large soilturn draped over their shoulder. Nearby Undallin stood with their siblings. And just a meter away an old retty, slumped over their staff held firmly in both hands, looking down at him.

Warin got to his feet. "Ollahnah," he said to the impression. "Joolid." He reached for his head. "I don't have my headset with me. If I knew you would be here, I would have brought it."

But the impression didn't speak, did not move. Warin took a step toward them, but somehow he wasn't any closer. He took another step, reaching out with his hand for their arm. He still could not reach them. He thought they were right there, right in front of him. But somehow they were as distant to him as the mountains beyond the village.

Warin lowered his hand, nodding slowly. "You're not really here," he said. He looked around the area. "None of you are. You're all gone. I forgot." He looked down at his feet. "I'm sorry. There was nothing I could do. I wanted to help but it was too late." His eyes started to well with tears. "It's not fair. It didn't have to happen. We could have stopped it. Could have saved all of you. But we didn't. We let you all die."

He sobbed deeply, still looking down, unable to face them anymore. "I wish you could understand me."

He felt something very soft, cold, brush his cheek. He looked up. Ollahnah had reached out to him with their hand. The native stared into his eyes. Warin felt no recrimination, no animosity in their face. They were sad, but they didn't blame him. The old native turned their head slowly, letting each of their eyes look at Warin directly. The old native pinched his cheek and smiled. Just like his grandfather used to do. The old native stood upright and walked away.

The others passed by him as well, brushing up against him as they did. Many nodded at him. Their hands were cool against his skin and sent a shiver up his spine. As the last one passed by Warin turned around. In the distance he could see a cloud of them moving off together.

He followed after them as the procession led out the side of the village and down the slight slope. He stood by the fence, watching as each of them separated from the mass and took up a spot in the field. They disappeared over the mound of dirt where their body lay. Soon enough all were gone.

He felt a heavy, stone-like hand on his shoulder. He turned

around to see the giant dark obsidian native standing behind him. Their black eyes focused into little globes of reflected starlight looking down on him.

"You've come to see the end?"

The figure gestured with their staff down into the field. Warin followed where it directed to a small corner of the field, somewhat apart from all the others.

"What is it?" he asked. "I don't see anything."

The figure gestured again. Warin looked closer. There was a small, rectangular outline in the ground, with a pile of dirt next to it. An unfilled grave.

Warin shook his head at the figure, backing away. "But I'm not dead."

The figure seemed to contemplate that for a moment. It turned to look up to the mountain where the observation post was, then back down at him. Its smile suddenly felt very unnerving.

Warin tripped on a tree root and fell onto his back, sending a sting of pain up his spine sharp enough to get through the numbness. He let out a small yelp at the pain, but that did not help much. He rolled over onto his stomach to take the weight off his spine. That helped more.

As he lay there wincing in the pain, his head facing the ground, bare human feet passed by his eyes. Then another pair. And another after that. He turned his neck to follow the feet, up bare calves and backside, up to the shoulders. When he reached her head, she turned to look at him vacantly, and then back ahead. She and the others kept going past the figure and down into the field.

The figure reached down and held out its hand to him. Warin stared at it.

"But I'm not dead," Warin repeated.

The figure nodded at him. "Not yet," it said. "You should come back here when you're near. We have a place for you. With us."

Warin ran, wildly, across the empty village. He fell many times, only to get back up and keep going. Suddenly he felt delirious, in a panic. He had no idea of a destination in his head. Just away from those fields, that figure. He could feel its stone hand on his shoulder still, the icy voice in his ears, and it spurred him on as he tried to escape it. He soon grew exhausted, sucking in the air, barely able to keep up his fearful pace.

He came to the edge of the grove and dived straight in. Even in the total blackness he kept going. He bounced off trees, got whipped in the face by low branches, turned around many times. His foot came down awkwardly on a tree root and he stumbled and fell hard against the ground, knocking the wind out of himself. He clutched at his stomach with his hand as he squirmed on the ground, letting out pained cries. He couldn't bring himself to stand anymore. He crawled to the side of a tree, resting his head on the rough bark, grasping at the ground beneath him, trading the utter black of the grove for his eyelids, and passed out.

Sixteen

THE SKY ABOVE was blinding beyond the silhouette of branches and trees when Warin opened his eyes. He squinted and brought his arm up to his face for shade. Slowly he came to his senses and saw where he was. Back in the grove, lying on the ground, his head somewhat elevated, nestled in the dirt between two roots. It was morning again.

He sat up with great effort, pushing off against the tree behind him. He rested back against the side of it, his head swimming for a moment before settling. He coughed loudly, racking his whole torso. When it subsided he took short breaths to keep from coughing again. He looked around. Definitely back in the grove. To his left he could see the edge of the trees and bits of the village homes beyond it. Looked like he hadn't run as far into the trees as he had thought.

He pulled a tablet out of his pack at his waist (thankful it was still there) and dropped it in his mouth. As it dissolved on his tongue, he tried to put the fragmented flashes in his head together into a coherent memory of what happened. Some of it made 'sense', but a lot of it, as much as he tried, didn't seem to fit together at all. As if they came from someone else and he had observed from a distance. And whatever logic there was to any of it was completely lost.

He shook his head with a sigh. Such a stupid night.

Warin stumbled through the trees, leaning heavily on their trunks as he passed by them. After a few minutes he found the path, and a few minutes after that was back at his campsite. He sat down heavily on the stool stump again, out of breath. His stomach felt like one great air bubble. He realized he had skipped breakfast when he had left the observation post, so hadn't eaten anything besides that damn leaf in over a day.

He opened his pack and took out a protein bar, tearing off the wrapper with his teeth and inhaling it. He immediately started to feel better as he grabbed another one. Not quite at full strength, but functioning. Enough to get through the day. After he finished the second bar he grabbed a new set of clothes, or at least a set that was not as ragged and dirty as the ones he had blindly run through the woods in, and changed.

He disassembled and packed up his tent and tied its compressed bundle down underneath the solid case on his pack. He grabbed the few remaining things around, stuffed them into his pack, and closed it shut. There was no space for the figurine, so he tied it to the back of his pack with some rope, doubling over it a few times to make sure it was secure. When he was done he slung the pack onto his shoulders, hopping in place once or twice to get reaccustomed to its weight. He looked around the area for anything he might have missed. Seeing nothing, he grabbed Rek and Lil's packs in each hand by their handle loops and headed off.

The two extra packs were heavy and cumbersome, and he had to stop twice to rest his arms. Fortunately, once he got out from the trees and onto the cobblestones, he could drag them behind him on their corner wheels.

The sound of the wheels on the stones was deafening, and echoed about the empty space. At the well he stopped to take a long drink and then fill his canteen, looking around furtively as he did. Memories of the night before kept superimposing themselves on the day around him now, and it left him feeling like there was someone nearby, right outside his view, looking at him. Dav, that native survivor with him? No, it wasn't them. It wasn't anyone. He knew it was his imagination playing with him. The village was just as empty as it had been the morning before. But he still hurried his pace away from the well and on out of the village gates. He turned to look back to the village only once, as he walked down the dip in the road, to watch it slowly disappear behind him.

It was well into the afternoon now, and the ambient sounds of the fields and forests around him came to life the farther he got from the village. Random clicks and chirps of small animals, a distant growl of something larger, mingled with the sound of grass swaying in the wind coming down off the mountains. He had not realized how absent it all had been from the village, as if life itself was unwilling to step foot near it anymore. He started to feel relieved to be away from the village despite himself.

He decided he was going up to the orbiting station and board *Ignacio* immediately when he got back. He could pack the few personal items of his in a few minutes, maybe say some quick goodbyes, head up to the launchpad, grab a shuttle, and just go. He'd had enough of the planet. It was time to move on. He imagined himself in a couple of hours, sitting in a nice seat in the crew lounge, staring down at this world as he sipped a stiff drink, leaving all that had happened the last few days behind.

He turned the corner in the road and stopped dead in his tracks. The jeep was gone.

He stood the extra packs on their ends and approached the side of the road where he was certain he had left it. The impressions of the tires in the dirt at the edge of the road led into grass pressed down in two even lines going off across the field.

He tapped his earbud. "Call Dav," he said in an exasperated tone. He didn't hear the computer voice in his ear responding. There was nothing at all. "Call Dav," he repeated more forcefully, emphasizing both syllables. But there was still nothing. He tried the others in turn, but nothing got a response of any kind from the network.

He took the earbud out and looked at it. Maybe it was damaged. He had been wearing it last night. But these things were supposed to be very durable—shock-resistant, water-resistant. They'd be worthless in the field otherwise. Even as hazy as last night still was, he couldn't think of anything he had done that could have broken it.

He took his pack off his back and laid it down in front of him. He unzipped a side sleeve and took out his pad, swiping his finger across it to bring it to life. A large working symbol rolled on the screen. That was itself concerning. The connection to the observation post should be instantaneous. After nearly a minute of the swirling circle, it went away instantly to be replaced with large, bold red letters: *NETWORK OFFLINE*.

"Goddamnit," he muttered. He dropped the pad to his side and looked up the mountain. Nothing looked out of the ordinary up there. As if he would even see if something was from this far away. But it shouldn't be possible for the network to be down in the first place. Countless redundancies, backup relays to the orbital station on top of all those… the amount of things that would need to go wrong for the network to fail! Lil must have been neglecting her duties more than anyone thought.

He put his pad away and opened up the pack, taking out his pistol and strapping it to his waist. When that was in place he swung his pack back onto his shoulders. He looked behind him at Rek and Lil's packs where they rested. They were fine where they were. He wasn't carrying them up the mountain too. Let Lil and Rek come and get them themselves if they wanted them.

He started out across the field, walking in between the pressed-grass tracks of the jeep. He wasn't too worried about finding his way to the post on foot. It was a pretty straightforward route. And after a few kilometers he should be able to see it above well enough to not go astray. He sighed, thinking about a few kilometers. Uphill. Thank God he had filled his canteen.

If it wasn't for the nagging feeling in the back of his head that something was wrong, he might have been absolutely annoyed.

Seventeen

WARIN SCAMPERED UP the side of a steep outcropping of rock and arrived at the small flat plain above, just outside one of the base's emergency exits, late in the afternoon. He stopped and took off his pack, kneeling down next to it as he took a long drink from his canteen. The hike had not been as bad as he thought it would be, and he had made decent time, though his body was still feeling weary.

He sipped from his canteen as he looked at the entrance. It was a solid metal door, with rounded edges and a thick pressure-sealed border, recessed a meter into the rock wall, which rose above it at a sheer incline all the way to the peak a half kilometer above. The larger garage door the jeep entered and exited from was around the side. Ten meters above the door and to the left were the observation post windows, an even row of four of them, cut straight out of the rock face as it curved around to the back. But instead of the normal glass, currently all four were closed off with slatted metal blast shields.

Warin stared at the blast shields, shaking his head. Those only come down in case of a natural disaster—an earthquake, hurricane, or some kind of volcanic activity. Or if there was a contagion, to keep one out or in. Basically any reason for a lockdown. He had never seen them deployed before in the whole time he had been stationed here.

He couldn't pretend this was just some technical difficulty. Something had definitely happened.

He grabbed his pack by the handle loop and carried it over to the door, dropping it against the rock face as he stepped into the recess. He looked through the tiny glass porthole in the door. Inside he saw the airlock, little more than a small, square antechamber. On the right-hand side the inner door was slightly ajar, leading to the hallway beyond it. In the small crack of the opening he saw flashing red in the otherwise dim light in the hallway.

He turned to the access panel embedded into the rock to the right of the door. He placed his hand on it, spreading his fingers wide. After a moment the pad flashed white and then blue. Thankfully that seemed to be functioning. Basic icon commands appeared in the area to the left of his hand. Warin pressed the open function and stepped back from the door. There was a loud click, and then another, but then nothing. The access pad started beeping. *CANNOT OPEN DOOR MECHANISM NONFUNCTIONAL* flashed in red letters on the screen.

Warin scratched the back of his scalp. He didn't actually expect the door would open, not if the base was in lockdown. He had only tried it to rule it out. But he thought it wouldn't have opened because he couldn't override the lockdown, not because it was malfunctioning.

He turned back to the porthole and looked through, standing on his toes and pressing the side of his face flat against the right side of the door. Looking downward, he was just barely able to see the access pad inside the airlock. Or what was left of it. The pad was smashed to pieces, its surface broken into shards, the lower corner hanging off below it by a single wire.

Warin leaned against the door. Nonfunctional. But not as

in *malfunctioning*. As in physically broken. Which meant the door would have to be opened manually. Which he couldn't do from this side of it.

He pounded his fist on the door by his hip a couple of times. He needed to know what was going on.

Warin opened the side sleeve on his pack and took out his pad. He fished around more, grabbed a cable, and connected his pad to the access panel through a port on its side. There was no network, but he should still be able to connect directly. In theory, at least. He had never had a reason to try before.

He had partial success. With his access code he was able to get into most of the system, but he had no control from his pad. That was good enough for now. With any luck he'd at least be able to figure out what had happened.

He thumbed through various status screens, looking for problems. The radiation levels inside the base were fine. There'd been no fire or structural collapse. The seal on the lab was not compromised, so no bacteria or virus had escaped. Nothing at all seemed out of the ordinary.

Then he pulled up the environmental settings. And his spine went cold.

The air in the base was over eighty percent carbon monoxide.

It was not just in one section, or one level of the base; it was everywhere. It seemed impossible for it to have collected to such high levels like that. It would have taken hours to fill up the entire base—and done so without being detected. At some point last night, when everyone was sleeping? But it would have set off an alarm. Actually, he realized it had. He couldn't hear it out here through the thick door, but he had seen the flashing red light in the hallway through the porthole.

Why had nobody reacted?

He wasn't able to access the base diagnostics from his pad to find out more. For that he'd need to get to Lil's station on the observation deck. He could also likely fix whatever the problem was from there as well. Far too late for anyone inside.

He stepped back from the door. It had no handle or latch of any kind, and the seam was far too tight to try and wedge anything into it. Not that he could've budged it. The door was at least a half-meter thick. And the garage door around the corner didn't have an access panel. It opened from controls in the jeep and was otherwise even more impenetrable.

He looked up at the observation windows, shaking his head. When everyone inside was suffocating to death the system responded by sealing them in even more. But the slats over the windows were not as thick as the door was. Maybe a couple of centimeters. On the rock face he saw a path of handholds and small jags that could get him up to them. There was even a small ledge he could stand on right next to the windows. What to do when he was up there...

He took out his pistol from his holster and looked at it. Standard issue, short-burst plasma bolt, variable setting. And he hadn't fired it once, so fully charged. But he doubted it could work like an acetylene torch. The charge would be used up before he could get through half a slat. If it didn't blow up in his hand first.

Though maybe that could work. It's not like he had any other ideas.

He climbed up to the rock wall, and carefully walked along the ledge with his stomach firm against the rock to the windows. The bottom of the windows were about waist-high to him, and a half meter from the end of the ledge. He tapped on the metal slats, and they gave ever so slightly under his fingers. They were interconnected but not absolutely firm. Seemed they were more about protecting the glass from debris than being utterly impervious. One point in his favor. Between the frame of the window and the rock there was a tiny gap, only a few centimeters deep. He shoved his pistol into the gap at the corner and pressed it in tightly. Then he took a deep breath, set the pistol to overload, and hustled away as quickly as he could.

He climbed back down half the rock wall and then jumped the rest of the way, landing awkwardly on his knee. He hurriedly limped inside the recess for the door and sat down on the ground, knees to his chest and covering his head and waited, hoping he wasn't about to incinerate the whole area or start an avalanche that would bury him alive in the tiny little vestibule.

The explosion was deafening, and he felt it shake the rocks through his back. Many rocks, from tiny to bone-crushing, fell and bounced around on the landing outside the recess, as a dust cloud came swirling around and over him, covering him with dirt. By the time the echo of the explosion came back from the other side of the valley, the cloud was already starting to dissipate, and the larger rocks had stopped falling. Warin didn't move until the ringing in his ears was a dull whir.

He took a quick peek from his hole upward, ready to dart back in at the slightest sense of alarm. Everything was still. He gingerly took a step out, shaking out his still-sore knee, his eyes still on the rock face. He saw no sign of imminent further rockfall or collapse all the way up to the peak. He turned his attention to the windows. White smoke billowed out from the corner where his pistol had just been, so it was hard to be sure, but he thought he saw bent and warped metal.

He climbed back up to the window. The lower three slats had been ripped from the side and bent inward, creating a small hole. The glass behind the slats had completely shattered, and he could see it on the floor inside, glinting in the flashing red light of the alarm. It would be tight, but it should be enough for him to get through.

He took out two oxygen tablets from his bag and popped them into his mouth. He then tossed the bag in before him. He leaned down to the hole, reached in on both sides, and pulled his head through. He pushed his arms in farther in front of him, working his shoulders in, twisting clockwise as he pulled. His feet left the ledge and dangled straight down behind him, and he braced for the sudden weight. He kicked in the air and pulled himself farther in. A sharp pain stung him in his armpit, as a jagged piece of the slat dug into his side. He ignored it and pulled himself in to his waist. He leaned his torso downward to the floor, forcing his hips through, after which his legs slipped past effortlessly, and he somersaulted to a stop on the floor of the observation deck.

He lay on the floor motionless, collecting himself for a long time, staring up at the flashing red light on the ceiling. The alarm still going off. There had been no one to shut it off. The rhythmic pulse of it started to mesmerize him, and his eyelids started to get heavy. He felt if he wanted, he could drift off right then and there, even with the little bits of glass digging into his back. He shook himself. No, he had to keep going. He still had to clear the air. He rolled onto his side and got to his feet.

He sat down at Lil's station and woke it. Thankfully, she was logged in. Up came the alert for the carbon monoxide, in big, flashing red letters. He started to reach out for it to tap it off, when he noticed down in the corner of the display a mute icon bolded. He realized for the first time that the room was quiet. The alert had no siren. On impulse, he tapped the icon. Suddenly the alarm siren wailed in his ears. He jumped at the suddenness of it, surprised, and tapped the alert to shut it down. The siren and the flashing red light stopped.

He stared at the display, shaking his head. You could sleep through a flashing red light. Not the siren. "Damn you, Lil," he muttered to himself. He set the thoughts aside. He wasn't finished. He brought up the environmental controls for the base.

The first thing he saw wrong was that the air scrubbers had been disabled, and he turned them back on. The CO levels started to drop. But not quickly. He looked for something else out of place. And he found it: the air circulation was compromised. Sensors showed that the system was pumping the heating system exhaust instead of oxygen out of the vents throughout the whole base. Somewhere, the lines had been crossed. He brought up the base diagram and highlighted the air pipes. Everything was fine in the basement, where the atmosphere generators were, filtering in more oxygen to the planet's air to make it more human-friendly before circulating throughout the base. Those were working fine. It was just above that where it went bad, the level where the labs and garage were. The break happened there, right before it got to the first vent of the base proper.

He pulled up the security camera in the garage. Against the back wall a service panel had been pulled and was resting on the floor. Inside the opening in the wall he could see two thick tubes had been crossed.

He sat back from the desk, staring at the image on the screen. There was nothing he could do about that from here. He would have to fix that manually. And the CO levels were still in the seventies.

He rolled the chair across the floor to where his bag of tablets was and picked it up. He opened the bag and looked inside. He had seven left. He still felt fine, all things considered, but he popped two in his mouth and closed the bag. Five to get down there, fix the airflow, and then back up here to the window to ride it out. That should be enough.

Warin got up, went to the elevator, and pressed the button. But it never came. He pressed the button again. Still no elevator. He started to turn back to Lil's station but stopped. Even if he could get them back online, she could have done something physical to them too. The last thing he needed was to get stuck between floors. He moved to the emergency stairwell.

He could feel the effect of the thick carbon monoxide within one flight in the stairwell. His head started to feel just the slightest bit hazy. He hurried his pace downward.

He found Rek at the landing for the door exiting onto the living quarters level. He was lying on his side, his arm and part of his head propping the door open. Warin stopped to look down at him. His skin was a sickly shade of blue. His mouth was open and his tongue was sticking out, swollen and dark, his eyes glazed over and milky, half-rolled back into his head. He must have woken up at some point and tried to escape, but didn't make it more than a few meters from his quarters around the corner.

Warin moved on and exited at the lab level at the next landing.

The door opened on the level at the end of a small corridor, a few meters from the elevator. Opposite the elevator was the hallway that ran between the lab and the garage.

He took two more tablets as his head was starting to throb, and turned down the other hallway quickly. On the right were the floor-to-ceiling glass walls of the lab, with island workstations overfilled with equipment, and walls of shelves and refrigerated compartments for keeping samples in. Halfway down the hall was the one and only entrance to it, a double-doored hatch opened by a flywheel. Across from it on the left side was the entrance to the garage.

Warin glanced into the lab as he walked between the two. A ball of silvery, pulsing glitter caught his attention. It sat by itself on one of the workbenches over a work pad that glowed brightly, its surface dancing in and out of itself. Vaguely next to it he saw a display that looked to have some kind of progress bar on it slowly working up to one hundred.

He turned back to the corridor. He had no time to examine that further.

He entered the garage and walked up to the wall opening. The two cumbersome-looking hoses, one red and the other blue, bulged out from the wall as they twisted around each other. Both were almost as wide as his body and covered with a thin fabric-like skin that was ribbed by a metal ringed frame underneath.

His head was getting heavy. He blinked several times. He had to hurry. He loosened the gap brace of the first hose and pulled it free with a hard tug, leaving it dangling off to the side while he moved on to the other one. He wasn't sure which of the two was the air and which was the gas, but as long as he switched them back where they were originally it didn't matter. His vision started to get bleary as he pulled at the second one, which was stuck on something. He yanked on it harder, vaguely wondering if it would be a problem if it tore. He finally managed to get it free and shoved it up into its proper connection, fastening it tight. One down. He stopped and bent over for a moment, having a hard time keeping his eyes open. He woke himself with a coughing fit. He had to finish. With a grunt he roused himself, grabbed the first hose, pushed it into place, and fastened it down.

He wasn't sure if he was imagining it, but he started to feel better almost immediately. The fog lifted from his head and the wooziness faded. He reached into his pouch and took another tablet, just in case. He looked up at the air vent near the ceiling and smiled.

First things first. He had to get the network back online, contact the orbital station, and call for help. Hopefully whatever Lil had done to that was not irreparable. If it was, he'd have to wait till they noticed and came down themselves. He didn't like the idea of leaving Rek where he was, never mind wherever the others were, even Lil, but he needed to get help down here first. And it was a crime scene, so he probably shouldn't move anything—

The knife thrust to the hilt into his right side made his entire body stiffen. The searing pain shot through him like fire. He instinctively moved forwards away from it. But the knife and the pain moved with him, tearing at the edges of the cut, which sent even more fire through his body. His legs started to buckle underneath him, and he reached out for the wall to keep himself upright.

Vaguely he was aware of a hand on his shoulder. He looked down at it, and followed the slim arm back to its shoulder. He turned his head farther and saw a face underneath a helmet, from which two cold eyes stared back at him, the breath from the nostrils fogging up the glass faceplate.

Bela.

Warin fell to the ground in a heap.

Eighteen

WARIN OPENED HIS eyes and saw a limp hand palm-down on the pockmarked carved rock of the garage floor. It took him a moment to realize it was his own. Took even longer for him to be surprised to still be alive.

He lay on his face on the ground, his left hand up to his face, his right trapped underneath his body. His legs were folded up under his chest as if he had fallen over while kneeling. On his side where the pain was, his shirt stuck to his body and felt wet and sticky.

Where he was stabbed, he remembered. Where Bela had stabbed him.

He tried to push himself up with his one free hand, but the pain of movement sapped all the strength out of him, and he fell back down with a whimper. He tried again, this time bracing himself against it, and managed to get himself into a sitting position against the wall, careful to angle his back so his wound did not make contact with it.

He sat there wheezing, gaining back his strength, fighting to keep his eyes open. First thing was to find out how badly he was hurt. He reached down to his wound and gingerly touched the area. He could feel the gash in his skin beneath his shirt, about half the length of his pinky, and the blood pooling in the wound and dripping down his side. When he had been prostrate the fabric in his shirt had dried and stuck over the wound, slowing the bleeding, but with all the movement that had ripped and the cut was fully open again and flowing. He clamped his hand down as tightly on the wound as he could without making him pass out from the pain.

He looked around the walls of the garage. Above him to the left was the first aid kit. He rolled over onto his knees and, using the wall as a brace, slowly got to his feet, coming to rest hard against it on his shoulder. He slid along the wall and grabbed the kit, opening it against his chest. He grabbed a can of coagulant foam with his free hand and a bandage in his teeth, letting the rest of the kit fall to the ground.

The relief from the pain was almost immediate as he sprayed the whole area around his wound, as the foam had a numbing agent in it. Applying the bandage stopped the bleeding further. When he was done, he leaned back against the wall, his legs half-bent under him. His side was still on fire and the pulses of pain ran along every nerve in him with each heartbeat, but it was diminished at least, calmed enough that he could think more clearly.

He looked down at his side. His shirt and shorts were dark with drying blood. By his foot he saw a puddle bigger than his head. He had lost a lot of blood. And the bandage was probably only a temporary fix. He needed real medical attention from someone with more than just basic training.

That would have been Bela.

"Sorry, Lil," he mumbled to himself.

The air in the base was already clean, so that problem was over with at least. But he couldn't stay in here. He pushed himself off the wall and half-stumbled a few steps before gaining control again, and slowly shuffled to the door. Each footfall hurt and sapped his strength, but he pushed the pain as far away as he could. He reached for the door handle but stopped and looked around the garage. He was in no condition to defend himself. And Bela was somewhere on the other side of the door.

The firearms were under lock and key in the locker on the far wall. No way would he be able to get to any of those. He scanned the workbench the other side of the door from him, but didn't see anything more useful than a screwdriver. One of the longer ones could do, but not well. But he didn't see many other options.

He moved toward the bench to pick one up. When he did he noticed a metal pole leaning against the far side of the workbench. He stepped over to it. It was an ax from one of the forestry kits. Much better. He leaned over with a groan and lifted it by the end of the handle.

He opened the door and looked down both ends of the corridor, making sure it was empty before stepping out, carrying the ax near its head in his left hand. He closed the door behind him and stepped toward the elevator and stairwell.

Bela was in the lab staring at him.

She looked surprised to see him, her mouth half-open. She stood by the side of the workbench where the glittery ball was, one hand brushing the edge of the table near the knife resting on a bloody towel.

Warin glared at her and gripped the ax in both hands. He held it in front of his chest and stared her down, trying his best to look intimidating. Or at least not about to pass out.

Bela calmly walked over to the lab door keypad just the other side of the glass from him. Warin tensed as she came near. She stopped and glanced over at him. She smiled, tapping the glass a few times with her knuckle, and then shook her head, turning back to the keypad. She punched a few keys on the pad and there was a loud locking sound, and the lights bordering the door turned red.

She turned back to Warin and switched on the intercom. "I can't believe I missed every vital organ," she said to him.

Warin dropped the ax to his side and stepped up to the glass. "What did you do, Bela?"

"Thanks for getting the air back, though. That oxygen mask was starting to get uncomfortable." Bela turned away and walked back over to the workbench. "I've never stabbed someone before, you know. First time. So maybe screwing it up is understandable. But then again, I know human anatomy. I should be able to stab someone properly, so they go down and they stay down. It's almost embarrassing. CO is so much easier. And obviously more effective." She turned to face him. "Warin, the luck you've had the last couple of days—I really don't know whether it's good or bad."

"Bela," Warin repeated.

Bela sat down in front of the ball on her workbench. "I mean, first you weren't here last night. And I admit I was concerned when I found out. I had hoped you had gone up to the space station, though. Which would have been fine by me. You'd be safe in orbit, but you'd also be out of my hair. You wouldn't know anything was happening until it was too late. See, none of this is anything personal. So I thought, lucky you. But then when I saw the jeep was gone, I knew you'd gone down to the village instead." She laughed. "Why would you go back down there? It wasn't bad enough the last time?"

"Bela, please," Warin said. "Talk to me."

"I am talking to you." She ran her hand centimeters above the ball, making the electro field that surrounded it glow light blue. "So okay, you were down at the village, praying, rending your garments, lighting candles, or doing whatever you went down there for. I thought you probably had no plans to come back right away. At least not in time. Mind you, it'd be decidedly bad for you still being on the planet when I released this." She tapped the barrier around the ball. "You would have been better off getting gassed."

"What is it?" Warin asked.

Bela ignored him. "But there was nothing I could do about it. You were still here. Okay. Such is fate. Of course, just to be safe, I made sure that even if you did come back early you would never be able to get back in. I hadn't thought of something like that pistol overload trick of yours though. Or I didn't think you would be so stupid as to try it." She looked up at him, shaking her head as if disappointed. "Do you have any idea how flammable carbon monoxide is? This base was full of it and you're blowing things up? You could have brought this whole side of the mountain down on you with that little trick. Honestly, I was so apoplectic watching you do it, I could hardly believe what I was seeing. Fortunately for both of us the CO concentration was so high that it was well above its upper flammability limit—it was effectively too rich to ignite. Otherwise you could have vaporized the whole base and have screwed up everything."

"So I'm lucky?"

Bela nearly jumped out of her seat. "That's what I'm saying!"

Warin put his forearm against the glass. "Bela, please. What are you doing?"

"I'm making a point," she snapped. She turned back to the ball. "You want to know what this is? It's catalog number 4539-221C in the Ministry database. In the banned tech section. Technically known as D-99SRN. But you would know it by its colloquial name: it's a Coda Swirl."

Warin looked at the pulsing ball and saw it not as a ball but as the swarm of particles it was. "Nanites."

"Special nanites," Bela corrected. "Replication rate ten times normal. Quantum speed processing. Part organic, so impervious to EM pulse or any other form of computer hack. Took me forever to get it right; had to make the first one manually before I could write the program for the rest. Biomechanics isn't my strongest area. But the Ministry diagrams were very detailed. Much more than I would have thought they would be." She laughed. "You know, with the kind of detail they have in those files, you might have actually been able to make the vaccine and aerosol delivery system."

Bela turned back to the small nanite cluster. "This right here, this is just the seed. There are only about twenty billion of them here. When they're released out of stasis, they'll double that in just a few seconds. And keep going."

"You're going to release them?"

"That's kinda the point in making them, Warin. Right now, they're downloading their programming, their instructions into each and every one of these little monsters." She glanced at the display next to the Swirl. "Still has four percent to go. Ugh, this has literally taken all day." Bela walked over to Warin, who stood just the other side of the glass. "When they're fully programmed, yes, I'm going to release them. And they'll grow, and spread, and devour every single particle of organic matter on this planet. Every tree, every animal, every insect. Every person. As well as the atmosphere, the oceans, everything. Hell, some of the softer metals too, I think. And nothing will stop their growth except the cold void of space. They'll strip this world down to a dull, dead rock, and rip apart anyone or anything that tries to land here for a thousand years."

Warin stared at Bela. She looked back at him, her eyes wide and fiery, her nostrils flaring. She looked like a totally different person than Warin had ever seen.

"You can't," he stammered. "You can't do this."

Bela smirked. "Obviously I can."

"But all the life—"

"The rettys are already dead. And the lesser species will be as soon as the Ministry moves in. To make way for farming, mining, for settlements. They could have saved them, let us save them, but of course not. 'We can't become the arbiters of life and death in the galaxy.' We're just observers. All life is sacred unless it means lifting a finger. It's all a lie. They've just been waiting for something like this ever since this post was dug out of the rock, watching, keeping their hands off, hoping something would wipe out the natives so they could move in with their hands clean. Noninterference. Sanctity of life. It's a joke."

"What good does destroying everything do?"

"Because then nobody gets to have this planet. And if they really believed their bullshit, they'll all be fine with that."

Warin rested his brow against the glass, shaking his head back and forth. "I can't let you do this."

Bela snorted. "You can't stop me."

Warin stood up, bringing the ax up in both of his hands.

Bela looked at it and laughed. "This is tempered metallic glass, Warin. Ten centimeters thick. Even if you weren't slowly bleeding to death, you wouldn't be able to so much as scratch it with that. That pistol overload trick wouldn't even work. You'd need a far bigger explosion than that." Bela looked suddenly concerned for a moment and quickly turned away from Warin.

"Bela, please don't do this." Warin pleaded. "It's wrong. You know it's wrong."

Bela, still facing away from him, shook her head, looking around the room. "If I were you, I'd stop trying to talk me down and see how your luck finally turns out."

"What?"

"You heard me. Your luck. Whether it's going to finish the

day good or bad." Bela walked over to a nearby set of drawers and opened it. "The elevator is disabled, but the stairs go all the way up to the launching pad." She turned back to Warin holding a set of pliers. "Now, that's a lot of stairs, and I don't imagine it'll be easy in your condition, but you should be able to make it and be off in a shuttle before the Coda Swirl is ready." Bela glanced over her shoulder. "It just reached ninety-six point three-seven-six percent uploaded. So you have something like forty minutes. Maybe fifty. If you're lucky."

"Bela, listen to me…"

Bela walked back over to the lab's glass wall and jammed the pliers into the intercom speaker. It sparked and smoked as it died. She smiled at him and walked back over to her workbench to watch the Coda Swirl.

Warin stared at her for a long time. Bela never looked up at him, acknowledged him at all. She had nothing left to say.

He walked back around the corner to the stairwell, opened the door and stumbled through, coming to rest heavily on the railing. He looked up the center of the stairwell. The steps squared upwards, flight after flight, growing to a fine point far above. It was a lot of stairs, a thousand at least. But he could make it in forty minutes. Maybe. His body ached, and he felt increasingly weak, groggy, but if he could just make it to a shuttle above and launch, the autopilot could take over and he could happily pass out then.

He brought his foot down on the first step, and stopped. He didn't have to stop her. Why risk it? She gave him a chance and he should take it. He could be in orbit and safe before the world was destroyed. It wasn't up to him to do anything about it. He wasn't the arbiter of life and death.

He really needed to get started up those steps.

He imagined that swarm of nanites flowing down the side

of the mountain, eating away everything it touched. He saw a bool as it dissolved from the back to the front, getting out one scream before its insides were gone and its head fell limp before it too was absorbed. The surviving rettys looking upward in dismay as they were ripped to pieces. The village, the woods, the fields, the air and water, everything broken down to nothing. He felt sick.

There had to be something he could do to stop her.

The nanites were inert until their programming was fully uploaded. If he could shut the power down to the base before the upload was complete, then they would never deploy. He could do that up at Lil's station on the observation deck.

He shook his head. Bela would have already thought of that. She definitely had battery power for her station in the lab. At least enough to finish programming the Coda Swirl. She probably had been using it since he got in. To stop her, he'd have to get into that lab. And there was no way he could get through that glass. No, she had planned this out all far too well.

But had she? Her initial plan, sure, but him not being in the base last night with everyone else had thrown a wrench in things, and she had had to improvise a little. Disabling the door to try and keep him out. Sneaking up and stabbing him when he got in. Obviously not part of her original plan. Neither had been successful. Barricading herself in the lab was her last resort, her trump card. Effective as it was, there must be something he could do about it.

Maybe if he just had big enough of an explosion.

Warin walked back to the lab door, staring at Bela. She looked up at him curiously as he passed, but didn't appear alarmed at all.

He took the ax and jammed it into the flywheel on the door. Shoving it down tight. He looked over at her, still at her workbench watching him, and smiled. Now she wouldn't be able to unlock the door and get out of the lab to stop him.

The stairs hurt, even going down, and he leaned on the rail all the way to the basement, going slowly. At the bottom he pushed his way through the door and headed straight down the narrow walkway between the large physical systems, power, heat, water filtration, the large machines on both sides of him. It was almost like a different world down here, with big, physical machinery, the walls lined with pipes going back and forth between them. Not at all like the smooth and clean base above. The air was noticeably thicker and harder to breathe, and he had to stop to rest halfway along the walkway to regain his strength. It felt like the underworld down here. He had never stepped foot in this basement. Likely no one besides Lil had in years.

He reached the local control panel against the far wall and leaned over it. He closed all the release valves on the heating and power generators and raised their output levels. For a few minutes nothing seemed to happen, but then he saw the pressure levels rising. Too slow, he worried. How much time had it taken him to get here? His head was getting foggy and he couldn't be sure.

Then the overload started, the pressure levels rising quickly outside safety parameters. Lights started to flash all over the board. A failsafe tried to kick in automatically but he shut it down. He shut down all the failsafes he could find. He reached behind the control panel and ripped out the cords connecting it to the systems, and the control panel went dead. No stopping it now.

As he walked back toward the stairs, the alert siren went started to wail in his ears, the red light flashing.

Bela was fighting with the door in the lab, desperate to get out. When he shuffled by, she looked up and slammed her whole body against the glass, kicking it, pounding her fists and body, screaming silently at him. Her teary eyes were wild. Warin stopped for the briefest of moments and watched her, as her head flailed back and she screamed in utter frustration and anger. He thought he even saw a tinge of fear.

He nodded at her. "This is probably gonna be big enough," he said, and walked on to the airlock exit.

He closed the airlock door behind him and scurried away as fast as he could, which was not that fast at all, sliding down the rock outcropping on his backside, ignoring the pain from his side every time he landed on it. He had no idea how large an explosion this was going to be. Or how much time he had to get clear.

Down on the valley floor, he saw the small square of the distant village below. It was barely the size of a peanut at this distance, but it stood out in the purple fields. He smiled at the sight of it, for the moment forgetting its sad reality, too satisfied in his act to save it.

Warin got fifty meters away before the deafening boom burst his ears, the searing light blinded him, the fire burned him, and the concussion wave slammed him in the back.

Epilogue

HE REMEMBERED FLYING. Or tumbling in the air. Then hitting trees and falling down through the branches. Landing on rocks. He rolled for a while too, he thought. And he crawled, dragged himself forward one hand at a time. His legs weren't much help at all.

He passed out for a while. Then woke, and continued.

He couldn't breathe very well. He kept coughing up liquid. His left arm was stiff, would barely bend. He couldn't move his hand, bend his fingers, make a fist. It seemed to have fused together in some way. He couldn't see well enough to tell, although he was sure he didn't want to anyway. It was still enough to pull him forward along the ground. And that was all that mattered right now.

He passed out again. Then woke, and continued.

Everything was in pain. But it was distant, someone else's maybe. Or perhaps just the various nerves screaming were so numerous that they canceled each other out, and left him feeling dulled, just the constant background sensation of his existence.

Wake up, continue.

The suns fell and it grew dark and cold. Or it should have been cold. He thought it should be. But he didn't feel it. And the darkness did not matter because only one of his eyes worked and it was dim all the time anyway. He kept crawling.

He passed out. Then woke and cried for a long time. After that, he continued.

It started to rain. And it was welcome. The drops were a relief on his back, cooling his skin. He turned over and opened his mouth to it. It filled quickly. Too much. He turned his head to his side and coughed it back up.

He decided to stay here, under the rain. It was good enough. And the strain of crawling was just too much. He didn't remember where he had been trying to get to anyway.

A long time later it was bright out. And he was flying again. No, not flying. He felt strong arms underneath his shoulders, his legs. His head bounced up and down. He was being carried. He looked up. The suns shone right into his eye. In front of the suns was a black shadow. It paid no attention to him.

He passed out.

THE NEXT TIME he woke he was in a cot, inside a large domed home. His sight was better. He could see the curve of the roof and the scrawled pictures above him. Though only with the one eye. He felt tight bandages over the other side of his face. He lifted his head off the cot to look around. His left arm was wrapped tightly up to his shoulder and laid across his chest. A blanket tucked him in at the waist, and he saw the outline of his legs. They looked wrong, but he wasn't sure exactly how. It was strange. He felt nothing.

The shadow appeared in the entryway. It strode over to his side and turned into a retty, a young, somewhat tired-looking one. Warin had met them before. Helluna. They knelt down to him, placing one of their hands on his shoulder.

"You should see the other guy," Warin said, trying to smile, only managing to cough a little.

Helluna patted him gently and reached to a table beside the

cot for a cup. They lifted Warin's head up with their hand while they helped him take a drink.

"Thank you," Warin said. "I take it you brought me down from the mountain?" The native stared at him. "Amazing that you found me," Warin said. He passed out again.

When he awoke it was darker, and Helluna was still at his side. The native looked down at him as his eye opened.

"Looks like I stopped her," he said. "I must have. We're still here. You're here, at least. I don't know where I am." Warin took a deep breath, stifling another cough. "I could have walked away. Just left. Nobody would have blamed me. I'm not the arbiter of life and death, you know. I'm sure even you would have understood." He paused, closing his eye. Helluna watched him patiently. "Though, maybe I guess I wouldn't have. I don't know. I just couldn't let her do it." Warin reached for Helluna's hand resting on the side of the cot. "You'll be all right now," he said to them.

Helluna looked down at his hand, then covered it with their own. They nodded to him.

Warin smiled at the native. "These are some fine bandages. Really solid work. But I don't suppose you know anything about internal medicine."

A severe coughing fit came over Warin that he could not suppress. He doubled over under it, spraying red mist all over his chest. A little dribble of blood trickled out the side of his mouth.

Helluna wiped his mouth with a cloth. *Rest now, friend Warin,* they said to him. *Rest. You are with us now.*

Warin closed his eyes, finding it easy to sleep. He didn't register that he had understood what Helluna had said to him.

THE HIGH NOON suns warmed the skin of his entire body as he woke one last time. He felt the soft ground on his back, heard the wind in the trees. Somewhere in the distance an animal cried. He raised his head and looked at himself. His bandages were gone. So were his clothes. He was not alarmed by this.

He looked over to his side and saw the fields. Row upon row of short, rectangular mounds stretched out to the back fence. The villagers. He looked over their graves slowly, methodically, row by row. He saw how uniform each was, the same size, same depth of very neat and orderly rows, like bricks in a wall, how they rose over the ground only a few centimeters at their height. He noticed how the farther back he looked, the lighter the dirt of the graves became, having had more time to dry in the sunlight than the closer, newer ones. Their bulges seemed to be flatter as well. In the very far rows it was hard to see the graves at all. Within a few more days, a few more rainfalls, and they all would blend in completely.

Above his head over in the near corner, Helluna was busy digging another one. They were almost up to their knees inside the hole.

Warin cleared his throat, which led to a cough. Helluna looked over at him. "I don't know how to tell you this," Warin said. "But I'm not actually dead yet." He coughed again. "Though I suppose it's got to be any moment now."

Helluna stepped out of the grave and walked over to Warin. They sat down next to him and took his hand in theirs. Warin looked up at them, squinting at the suns. "I suppose you just wanted to get a head start," he said. "That's all right." He looked over at his grave, then up at the native. "It looks deep enough now. All ready for me. Sorry I'm throwing your schedule off."

Helluna shook their head slightly, letting each of their eyes stare at him in turn.

Things started to feel faraway, numb. He still felt Helluna's hand in his, the grass on his back, heard the wind, saw the native watching him, but from an ever-increasing distance. The pains of his body slowly melted away, and he felt he could relax a tenseness that he had been carrying forever. The world grew dark, which confused him for a moment because he wasn't closing his eye.

"It's a nice spot," he mumbled. "Among friends."

After a time, Helluna carried Warin's body over to his grave and gently placed him in it.

About the Author

A.T. Sayre has been writing in some form or other ever since he was ten years old. From plays to poems, teleplays to comic books, he has tried his hand at pretty much every medium imaginable. His work has appeared in *Analog Science Fiction and Fact*, *Haven Speculative*, *Aurealis*, *Andromeda Spaceways*, and *StarShipSofa*. His first short story collection, *Signals in The Static*, was published in May 2024 by Lethe Press. A more detailed list of his publications can be found at www.atsayre.com/fiction.

Born in Kansas City, raised in New Hampshire, he lives in Brooklyn and likes to read in coffeehouses.